Eugene Onegin

WALTER ARNDT was born at Constantinople in 1916. After studying economics and political science at Oxford University, he moved to Poland for postgraduate work in economics and the study of Slavic languages. In 1939 he volunteered for the Polish army and served in the autumn campaign and later in underground work in Warsaw. Between 1942 and 1945 Mr. Arndt was active in military and economic intelligence with the U.S. Office of Strategic Services in the Aegean theater. After several years in UN refugee relief work, combined with an instructorship at Robert College, Istanbul, he emigrated to the United States. Until 1956 he taught classics and modern languages at Guilford College and The University of North Carolina, where he took his doctorate in linguistics and classics. After Ford fellowships at the University of Michigan and Harvard, Mr. Arndt held successive appointments in Linguistics and Slavic studies at The University of North Carolina and guest professorships at Münster, Germany, and the University of Colorado, Boulder. He left The University of North Carolina in 1966 as chairman of the Department of Linguistics, Slavic, and Oriental Languages to take up a professorship in Russian Language and Literature at Dartmouth College.

Arndt's verse translation of Pushkin's *Eugene Onegin* was published in 1963 and awarded a Bollingen Prize that year. His English anthology of Anna Akhmatova's verse and his complete verse translation of Goethe's *Faust* in the metric forms of the original came out in 1976. He has also published other works on Pushkin and monographs on linguistic theory and glottochronology.

Current work includes a novel; a cycle of Mandelshtam poems; a bilingual anthology of the poet-painter Wilhelm Busch (the last on a Guggenheim fellowship); a verse translation of Pushkin's dramatic poem *Poltava* (as a fellow of the National Endowment for the Humanities); and a collection of Pushkin's poetic oeuvre in English.

ALEXANDER PUSHKIN

Eugene Onegin

A NOVEL IN VERSE

Second Edition, Revised

THE BOLLINGEN PRIZE TRANSLATION
IN THE *ONEGIN* STANZA
EXTENSIVELY REVISED,
WITH AN INTRODUCTION AND NOTES

by

WALTER ARNDT

CRITICAL ESSAYS BY
Roman Jakobson, D. J. Richards,
J. Thomas Shaw, and Sona Stephan Hoisington

A Dutton *Paperback*

E. P. DUTTON • NEW YORK

For information contact: E. P. Dutton, a division of New American Library, 2 Park Avenue, New York, N.Y. 10016

Library of Congress Catalog Card Number: 79-50763

ISBN 0-525-48311-X

Published simultaneously in Canada by Fitzhenry and Whiteside Ltd., Toronto

10 9 8 7 6 5 4

Second Edition

Grateful acknowledgment is made to the following for permission to use copyrighted material:

D. J. Richards, "Russian Views of Pushkin," appeared as part of the Introduction in *Russian Views of Pushkin*, D. J. Richards and C. R. S. Cockrell, eds. (Oxford: Willem A. Meeuws, 1976). Copyright © 1976 by Willem A. Meeuws; reprinted by permission of D. J. Richards and the publishers.

Roman Jakobson, "Marginal Notes on *Eugene Onegin*," *Pushkin and His Sculptural Myth*, John Burbank, trans. and ed. (The Hague and Paris: Mouton, 1975). Copyright © 1975 by Mouton & Company, N.V.; reprinted by permission of Roman Jakobson and the publishers.

J. Thomas Shaw, "The Author-Narrator's Stance in *Onegin*." Copyright © 1980 by J. Thomas Shaw; printed by permission of the author.

Sona Stephan Hoisington, "The Hierarchy of Narratees in *Eugene Onegin*," *Canadian-American Slavic Studies*, 10, No. 2 (Summer 1976). Copyright © 1976 by Canadian-American Slavic Studies, Arizona State University, Tempe; reprinted by permission of Sona Stephan Hoisington and the publishers.

Preface to the Second Edition

The fifteenth anniversary of publication offers a plausible, if tardy, occasion for cleaning, renovation, and adding-on. In the present case these take two forms: revisions, major and minor, in the body of the verse, and the addition of some illuminating critical commentary by Pushkin scholars to the small original apparatus of introduction and annotation. Any significant expansion of the chapter notes beyond the modicum useful to non-specialists was rendered supererogatory by the plethora of information, opinion, and, at times, bizarrerie on and off *Onegin* released in 1964 by V. V. Nabokov with his prodigious two-volume commentary—probably his most enduring, certainly his most endearing, opus. The present translation may be super-abundantly complemented by the boundless learning of Mr. Nabokov—who did not compliment it, however, except before its publication.

The emendations accumulated since 1963 affect perhaps one-third of the stanzas in some chapters, one-twentieth over the whole. They were prompted in a few instances by little quantum jumps in understanding of the poet's intent or effects; more often by long-felt distress over syntactic or metric gadgetry, semantic evasions, lexical infelicities (not to mention some hardy misprints, like the inglorious one of the bear in Tatyana's dream who has been on her *tail*—for *trail*—intermittently since 1963); sometimes, not often enough, by newly perceived shortcuts toward the simplicity and sparkle of the original. *Eugene Onegin* was my earliest major venture (after parts of Mickiewicz's Polish idyll, *Pan Tadeusz*) into verse translation in the proper sense of the term; which is, of course, *Umdichtung*, "form-true remaking" (from a single translator-poet's familiar habitat in both the old and the new linguistic medium) of the poem's seamless whole—its "shape-content continuum." Twenty years and several larger enterprises later I sense that I am a better poet, certainly a more skillful and fastidious journeyman in the intricate matching and meshing crafts involved. I hope it shows here and there in the revision.

The inclusion of several essays by distinguished contemporary critics and scholars should add very significantly to the reader's understanding of this unique work, its author, and the culture in which it is so deeply and permanently embedded. I want to express my warm thanks to Roman Jakobson, David Richards, Thomas Shaw, and Sona Hoisington for their gracious willingness to release their work for the present purpose; and to the editor and publishers of *Canadian-American Slavic Studies,* Charles Schlacks and Arizona State University; Messrs. Mouton, publishers of Roman Jakobson's "Marginal Notes on *Eugene Onegin*" in *Pushkin and His Sculptural Myth;* and Messrs. Willem A. Meeuws, publishers of *Russian Views of Pushkin,* edited and translated by D. J. Richards and C. R. S. Cockrell, for granting their kind permission to reprint all or part of the above pieces.

WALTER ARNDT

Hanover, New Hampshire
1978

Preface to the First Edition

Eugene Onegin, Pushkin's own favorite and central in his poetic output, is one of the outstanding and seminal works of Russian literature. It is a brilliant evocation of its own time and place, inaugurating realism in the Russian novel, yet it is also intimately related to eighteenth-century French literature and to Byronism. Extending to nearly 400 stanzas of sonnet length with an original and unvarying rhyme pattern, it is made up in about equal parts of plot, of delicate descriptions of nature and milieu, and of digressions in the Byronic manner.

The novel is concerned, as Vladimir Nabokov has put it, with "the afflictions, affections, and fortunes of three young men—Onegin, the bitter lean fop; Lensky, the temperamental minor poet; and Pushkin, their friend—and of three young ladies—Tatyana, Olga, and Pushkin's Muse." The setting is Russia in the 1820's; the scene shifts from the capital to the country, to Moscow, and back to St. Petersburg, with the author, by way of comment and excursus, subtly moving in and out of the focus of interest. There are superb vignettes of nature in various seasons and moods and of the precocious hedonist's cycle of pleasures and dissipations, ending in disenchantment and emotional aridity; there are the authentic physical and mental settings of rustic squirearchy and metropolitan society; a dream, a duel, and two climactic epistles celebrated in Russian literature; and a wealth of autobiographical asides and varied digressions—literary, philosophical, romantic, and satirical—which add to the multiplicity of moods, levels of discourse, and themes.

Four English verse translations have preceded this one in the 125 years since Pushkin's death. Three appeared in or near the centenary year, 1937; only one, that by Babette Deutsch printed in Avrahm Yarmolinsky's voluminous Pushkin anthology, is still in print. For the present new translation, no elaborate exegesis was intended, and only enough chapter notes have been provided to clarify references to literary and cultural matters, private allusions, etc. It is not aimed primarily at the academic and literary expert, but at a public of English-speaking students and others interested in a central work of world literature in compact and readable form.

I have consulted a variety of editions and used some arbitrary discretion in including or omitting stanzas and fragments variously treated there. The original Chapter VIII, dealing with Onegin's travels in Russia, is not included despite its many felicities, as I believe that in the interest of the harmony of the whole, Pushkin was wise in omitting it from later editions. This is even more true of the scattered and uncertain fragments of the original Chapter IX concerning Eugene's supposed involvement with the Decembrists. I am indebted to several previous commentators and editions, English and Russian, especially those by Professor Oliver Elton and Professor Dmitry Čiževsky, for note material. I also owe a debt of gratitude for helpful comments to friends and senior colleagues in the field of Russian literature and prosody at Harvard University and elsewhere, notably Roman Jakobson, Michael Karpovich, Renato Poggioli, Hugh McLean, Boris Brasol, Ernest J. Simmons, Leon and Galina Stilman, Ralph Matlaw, and Richard Gregg. Several emendations were suggested by Vladimir Nabokov's criticisms at various times.

Acute accents are used to indicate stress in Russian names that might otherwise be misread; elsewhere the iambic meter should be the reader's guide.

WALTER ARNDT

Contents

Introduction

Eugene Onegin (1823–31) is to most Russian readers Pushkin's outstanding and most characteristic work, the title that first comes to mind when Pushkin's name is mentioned. Some critics single out other, smaller works as gems of perfection, as Mirsky does for *Tsar Saltan,* and certainly a strong case may be made for several of these as unsurpassable highlights of genius. Yet in *Eugene Onegin* the slow virtues of the novel so beguilingly combine with the epigrammatic fire of the discursive poem, with the pathos of a psychologically plausible affair of the heart, and the charm of genre painting that it must be accorded the prize even in a poetic output of such astonishing and sustained perfection. *Eugene Onegin* was Pushkin's own favorite; almost ten years in the writing and revising, it reflects the author's own gradual growth in organic changes of literary mood which create an extraordinary illusion of depth and perspective. Here was a new art form in Russia—a novel, and, what is more, a novel in verse, "which is a devil of a difference," as Pushkin himself remarked in a letter to Vyazemsky. The authorized version contains eight cantos, or chapters, as Pushkin calls them, of fifty stanzas each, totaling some 5,600 lines of verse. The invariable 14-line unit, celebrated as the Onegin stanza but rarely attempted since, is a thing of intricate and varied beauty for which there is no precise precedent in metrics. Its main constituents are iambic tetrameters, a well-known metric unit in classical and modern verse; but these units are combined and interlaced in a sonnet-like stanza of a delicate and complex balance. The four iambic feet of each line incorporate the compact or mellifluously long, but predominantly single-stressed, Russian words in a constantly varying pattern, unlike any effect achievable in a language with subsidiary stresses, and they follow one another in the following intricate rhyme scheme:

IV. 41

a	Through frigid haze the dawn resurges;
B	Abroad the harvest sounds abate;
a	And soon the hungry wolf emerges
B	Upon the highway with his mate.
c	The scent scares into snorting flurries
c	The trudging horse; the traveler hurries
D	His way uphill in wary haste.
D	No longer are the cattle chased
e	Out of the byre at dawn, the thinning
F	Horn-notes of cowherds cease the tune
F	That rounds them up again at noon.
e	Indoors the maiden sings at spinning
G	Before the crackling pine-flare light,
G	Companion of the winter night.

Lower-case letters denote feminine rhyme; capitals, masculine rhyme. Thus we discern three quatrains of differing rhyme schemes, followed by a couplet which neatly rounds the stanza off and invites some epigrammatic or aphoristic conclusion; such epigrams or sardonic tag lines abound in the poem. One may go further and say with Čiževsky that the typical stanza contains in its microcosm a proposition, an exposition elaborating or exemplifying it, and a peroration summing up the argument with a final flash of wit or persiflage. Obviously a great deal can be done with, and in, a stanza of this length and variety; and Pushkin does it all.

Eugene Onegin spans Pushkin's most creative years; it became his magnum opus. Ten chapters were planned, the ninth to deal with Eugene's travels after the fateful duel, the tenth with his part in the Decembrist conspiracy. Fragments of this last chapter are extant, written in Pushkin's private cipher and not completely decoded. The ninth chapter is fragmentary also, but is often printed as an appendix to modern editions. The work was published chapter by chapter at irregular intervals, the first shortly after the southern exile in 1825, the rest, through Chapter VI, in magazines and almanacs, with some fragments and individual stanzas later omitted by the author. Chapter VII did not appear in a separate edition until early 1832. In June 1833 the novel was published as a whole for the first time, designated as the second edition by modern count. The second complete edition, the third by our count, appeared shortly before Pushkin's death.

Pushkin originally called *Eugene Onegin* "a novel in verse in the manner of Byron's *Don Juan*," and in the preface referred to it as a satirical work. Later he denied in a letter that it was like *Don Juan* or had anything satirical in it. This reflects not so much inconsistency as the slow growth and change of the novel over the years, the indefiniteness of the original plan, and the quasi-spontaneous evolution of the protagonists under Pushkin's hand. Tolstoy, in an anecdote told at second hand, relates that Pushkin spoke to someone of his "surprise that Tatyana turned Eugene down." Another time, when a sentimental lady expressed her hope that Eugene and Tatyana would be reunited, Pushkin is reported to have scotched the idea with the deprecating remark: "Oh no, he is not worth my Tatyana!"

The plot of the novel is very simple, but the loose form allows scope for a wealth of description and poetic excursus. Eugene and Tatyana are the only extensively drawn characters; the supporting couple, Lensky and Olga, are kept deliberately sketchy and conventional as foils to the others. About one third of the novel is concerned with the plot, another third with descriptive passages, the last third with digressions, such as Pushkin's reminiscences of theater and ballet experiences, literary or social polemics, gourmand revels, amorous recollections, and soliloquies on literary craftsmanship. It is also interesting to follow what has been termed the successive incarnations of Pushkin's Muse—his St. Petersburg beauty, his Lenore, his country miss.

The events of the novel are set in the time of Pushkin's young manhood, the early 1820's; the settings are St. Petersburg, the countryside of central Russia, Moscow, and (in the chapter of travels omitted by the author) distant parts. After an abrupt snapshot of the hero en route to his moribund country uncle, the plot begins with a brief flashback, flippantly describing the academic and mundane education of a playboy of the St. Petersburg *jeunesse d'orée,* his introduction to society with its elegant dissipation and breathless round of pleasures, and his gradual satiety and world-weariness, leading to his withdrawal to the country estate he inherited. There he is drawn into the rustic family circle of a typical squire of the period. The elder daughter of the house, the shy, bookish, unworldly Tatyana—a figure to conjure with in Russian literature—falls in love with him and writes him an ingenuous declaration, which is as enchanting today as it was five generations ago. In it, overcome and confused by a turmoil of feelings never before experienced outside of novels, she throws herself upon his mercy. Eugene is moved, but unresponsive. Too honorable to play her false, but too jejune of mind and drained of emotional energy to respond to her fresh ardor, he solicitously lectures her like a gentle older cousin, sighing that for him the days of love are over.

Meanwhile, Eugene's new neighbor and ill-matched friend, Lensky, a young poet moonstruck by German idealism, has won the volatile affections of Tatyana's sister, Olga, and become betrothed to her. After a party at which Onegin is playfully familiar with Olga in order to tease Lensky, his callow friend is deeply mortified and challenges him to a duel. Onegin, a seasoned duelist, out of foolish pride accepts before he can stop himself, and in the duel Lensky is killed. This tragedy wrecks the brief idyll, and Eugene leaves the countryside in greater disillusionment and self-torment than he had left the capital.

The plot now turns to Tatyana, her grief, her visit to Onegin's abandoned manor and library, and her family's resolve to take the despondent young misfit to the marriage market of Moscow, where, one gathers, she will be cajoled into marriage with a middle-aged dignitary. Onegin's restless wanderings are described in the original Chapter VIII, later excluded from the work after a large fragment had already been published. The new Chapter VIII, now the concluding canto, brings Eugene back to St. Petersburg, years after the crisis of Tatyana's rejection and the duel. At a brilliant ball he is stirred by the sight of a regally poised society beauty—his hostess, as it turns out; and in her he incredulously recognizes Tatyana. He is swept off his feet, his desultory search for purpose and meaning in life seems ended, and he implores her to renounce her marriage and station for his sake. She candidly admits that she loves him still, but despairs of turning back the clock, and steadfastly declines to betray her husband. This ends the story of a love out of phase and twice rejected, so curiously alien both to Romanticism and to the New Sensibility; and here the author wryly abandons his inadequate hero, the moody companion of his most creative years.

A brief structural analysis may help to illustrate the artful interweaving of plot, description, and digression:

Ch. I:	(Eugene's early life, worldly education, pursuit of of pleasure, satiety; his move to the country.)
18–20	Evocation of former glories of Russian theater and ballet, woven into Eugene's evening at the ballet and night at a ball.
29–34	Author "fades in" with nostalgic recollection of bygone pleasures and a zest now lost, leading to the famous lyrical digression on ladies' feet; recalls brief fictional friendship and kinship with Onegin, a shared longing for foreign travel.
55–60	Dissociates himself from Onegin in rhapsodizing on country life, which Eugene finds boring.

The claim of *Eugene Onegin* to be not only a unique mirror
of its author's mind and time, but also the first modern Russian
novel, is by no means absurd. It had an inestimable formative
influence on the course and complexion of the novelistic output
of the century. Not only in its palpable genre painting but in
the balance and climate of the Eugene-Tatyana relationship, the
great poem became the matrix of a distinguished line of Russian
novels, through Lermontov, Turgenev, Goncharov, and Tolstoy
to later writers. The contrast between a disoriented or disil-
lusioned, though gifted and sophisticated, man and an earnest,
candid, sweet-tempered girl long haunted the Russian literary
scene.

Pushkin treats his semi-autobiographical hero with gentle irony and detachment, but also with empathy and comprehension, as well he might. He comes to the conclusion that Onegin is to some degree the helpless child of his age, although he never hints, as later interpreters have willfully claimed, that Onegin was a member of a lost generation of frustrated brilliance, whom the autocratic regime and the failure of the Decembrist conspiracy had cheated of serious outlets for their creative energy. In the fine scene in Chapter VII where Tatyana visits Onegin's abandoned manor and tries to divine his character from his books, Pushkin sketches for us a fascinating little inventory of the Russian Byronist's mental furniture. While no author except Byron is actually named, we sense the presence of the literary ancestors of the *lishny chelovek,* the "superfluous man" of the Russian nineteenth-century novel, in the shape of Chateaubriand's *René* and Benjamin Constant's *Adolphe,* not to mention *Werther.* Not so much Tsarist repression as the ubiquitous literary *mal du siècle,* the individual's indolent disgust with society, might be made responsible for Onegin's failure and for the ineffectual heroes of the Romantic generation.

The author in *Eugene Onegin* plays a triple role—that of narrator, of an acquaintance of the hero, and of a character in the poem. This makes for a variety of levels and attitudes similar to that in Pushkin's maiden work, *Ruslan and Lyudmila,* and results in a lively interplay of plot, description, digression, and confession. For the virtue of looseness Pushkin is no doubt indebted to Laurence Sterne. As Byron had in *Beppo* and *Don Juan* found his way out of the narrower mold of *The Giaour* or *The Corsair* into Sterneian discursiveness, so Pushkin operates here deftly with constant shifts of focus and mood, with much metalinguistic and metaliterary verse, that is to say, sly discourse on lexical and poetic technique and on literary polemics, often cast in the form of chitchat with the reader. Yet Byron, with his outrageous rhymes and headlong descents into bathos, more than once appears to mock poetry itself, rather than merely the heroic or romantic mood in poetry; while at the core of Pushkin's mind there is a deep seriousness about one thing—verse—and an unremitting, though seemingly effortless, insistence upon its utmost precision and purity. Furthermore, *Don Juan,* of which *Eugene Onegin* has so often been mistermed an imitation, could not be imagined in a setting of nineteenth-century London society; one major dimension of it is the exotic background. Pushkin, for his part, shares with the reader a well-known, sometimes shabby, reality. There is not merely a sequence of anecdotes, monologues, and episodes strung on the undulating cord of the author's caprice, but also a real novelistic plot and dynamic character development in the two leading figures at least, and in miniature in many others.

Novels in verse were never achieved again, not even by Lermontov (cf. his *Sashka*), who experimented with the *Onegin* stanza; and the audacity of making everyday life into the stuff of novel and poem at the same time won the lasting admiration of the later realists, when they acknowledged their debt to Pushkin in their works and their eulogies.

WALTER ARNDT

Chapel Hill, North Carolina
1963

Russian Views of Pushkin

D. J. RICHARDS

From a literary, let alone a psychological point of view Pushkin is, like all great writers, a highly complex phenomenon. He was magnificently unique, but also a transitional figure in the development of Russian literature. His roots lay deep in the aristocratic French literature of the eighteenth century, yet he exercised a dominating influence on Russian nineteenth-century literature, of which he has been called the father-figure, even though much of this literature evolved as a conscious reaction against some of the poet's most cherished aesthetic values. His countrymen regard him as their national poet, yet outside Russia he is relatively unknown. And even among those Russian critics—the vast majority—who do not dispute Pushkin's eminence, there is a wide measure of disagreement over the precise nature of his artistic achievement and of his role in the history of Russian literature.

By descent, upbringing, and temperament Pushkin was an aristocrat (albeit an impoverished one) and moreover a member of the Russian aristocracy of the early nineteenth century when that class was dominated by the cultural values of the French *ancien régime.*

On his father's side the family traced its descent from a forebear who served with Alexander Nevsky in the thirteenth century, while Pushkin's earliest recorded ancestor on his mother's side, his maternal great-grandfather, the Ethiopian Ibrahim Hannibal, was a distinguished servant of Peter the Great who gave him among other rewards the country estate of Mikhailovskoye, which eventually came into the poet's possession. Although impoverished, Pushkin was no repentant nobleman. Throughout his life the poet possessed, it seems, an inborn sense of social superiority. Although in his mature years he would admit to having earlier adopted a somewhat exaggeratedly aristocratic pose in imitation of Byron, he never felt anything but pride and gratitude for his "600-year-old nobility."

From an early age Pushkin moved in the highest Russian social and intellectual circles. As a young boy he had been allowed to sit in at gatherings in his parents' house of some of the leading Russian *littérateurs* of the day. From the age of twelve to eighteen he was educated at the newly founded Lycée in Tsarskoye Selo where the most brilliant sons of the Russian nobility were to be prepared for posts of high responsibility in the service of the state. Even before leaving school he was admitted to membership of Arzamas, one of the leading literary societies of the period. Later he married a beautiful and socially eligible woman and, willingly or not, spent his last years in close attendance at the court of Tsar Nicholas I.

Pushkin's aristocratic background found expression not only in his writing but also in the style and panache of much of his way of life, from the precise elegance of his handwriting and the more casual elegance of his attire to the dashing vigor of his social life. In his youth Pushkin shared many of the young Onegin's foppish tastes and, like his hero, indulged himself in that exhausting round of dancing, womanizing, gambling, and dueling which was the fashion among young aristocrats of the period. Tolstoy, it is true, called Pushkin "a man of letters" [*literator*], assigning him disparagingly to the same class as Turgenev and Goncharov, in contrast with Lermontov and himself, but for Gogol the poet was very much a highly disconcerting man of the world who seemed to be frittering away his life and his genius at society balls.

During the early years of the nineteenth century when Pushkin's literary values were formed, Russian literature was a preserve of the aristocracy and Pushkin gladly associated himself with the aristocratic standards and attitudes which held sway. "We can be justly proud," he writes, for instance, to Bestuzhev

in 1825, "that though our literature yields to others in profusion of talent, it differs from them in that it does not bear
the stamp of servile self-abasement. Our men of talent are noble
and independent . . . our writers are drawn from the highest
class of society. Aristocratic pride merges with the author's self-
esteem . . ." And in the same year he wrote in a similar vein to
Ryleyev: "Don't you see that the spirit of our literature depends
to a certain extent on the social position of the writers . . . ?"

At the same time Pushkin's early literary triumphs seemed to
reflect that effortless superiority which has been held to be one
of the supreme distinguishing characteristics and virtues of the
ideal aristocrat. All Russians know, for instance, how Derzhavin,
the great court poet of Catherine II, was enraptured by the
schoolboy Pushkin's recitation of his *Reminiscences of Tsarskoye
Selo* and how five years later Zhukovsky, the leading poet of the
early nineteenth century, sent Pushkin his portrait inscribed with
the dedication, "To the conquering pupil from the conquered
master in memory of the notable day on which he completed
his poem *Ruslan and Lyudmila,* 1820, March 26, Holy Friday."

By the middle of the following decade, as writers and critics
from other classes (most notably Gogol and Belinsky) came to
the fore, the social flavor of the Russian literary world had
changed quite markedly, causing Pushkin some discomfort.
"There was a time," he writes, for instance, in 1834, "when
literature was an honorable and aristocratic profession. Now it
is a lousy market . . ." Though Pushkin was compelled to com-
pete in the lousy market in order to support himself and his
extravagant family, it is easy to sense where his literary and
social sympathies lay.

It is of course impossible to determine precisely the origins of
Pushkin's (or anyone else's) mature literary style. Doubtless
much derives from nature as well as from nurture—and neither
of these is susceptible to accurate measurement. However, if one
accepts that the values of his particular social environment exercised an influence on Pushkin's aesthetic judgments, then it
follows that the poet owed a considerable debt to France.

In Russian polite society at the end of the eighteenth and the beginning of the nineteenth century French aristocratic manners were imitated. The French language was spoken (many Russian nobles had only a defective command of their native tongue), and among the cultivated the literature of France was read more widely than that of Russia itself, while moreover much Russian literature was produced in imitation of French models. Pushkin was brought up to speak French as well as Russian and throughout his life he continued the practice of reading French literature, which he had begun as a boy in his father's extensive library. The poet's knowledge of French—which he used for much of his correspondence—was excellent, and indeed in a letter of July 1831 to Chadayev he claimed it was a more familiar language to him than Russian. According to Annenkov the poets dying words were spoken not in Russian, but in French ("Il faut que j'arrange ma maison").

The influence of the French language on Pushkin's prose was considerable. Gallicisms are found in his Russian and so much of the structure of his sentences was conditioned by French habits (and by a certain conscious imitation of Voltaire's style) that when Prosper Mérimée translated *The Shot* and *The Queen of Spades* he found that entire paragraphs went straight into his native language. "I think that Pushkin's prose construction is entirely French. I mean French of the eighteenth century," he wrote in 1849 to his Russian friend, S. A. Sobolevsky. ". . . I sometimes wonder whether you boyars do not first think in French before writing in Russian."

At the same time, Pushkin's debt to France was much more than a purely linguistic one. His immediate experience of French classical literature and his indirect experience of the culture of the pre-revolutionary French aristocracy as it found reflection in contemporary Russian society probably contributed much to that formal grace and that classically aristocratic spirit which are perhaps the distinguishing features of Pushkin's mature style.[1]

It is perhaps also worth noting at this point that Pushkin's knowledge of German was comparatively slight and, unlike many subsequent Russian nineteenth-century literary figures, he was not influenced to any significant extent either by the ideas or by the style of the German metaphysicians whose writings contributed so much toward shaping the cast of the Russian intellect during the second quarter of the century. To be more precise, he seems to have been actively hostile to this influence. "You reproach me concerning *The Moscow Messenger* and German metaphysics," he wrote to Delvig in March 1827. "God knows how much I hate and despise the latter, but what can one do? . . ."

In any event, whatever the precise origins of Pushkin's style, its essential characteristics are clearly marked and remain constant through all the vicissitudes of the poet's literary career and through all the many genres in which his work appeared. As Maurice Bowra put it:

> Pushkin is in fact a classical writer . . . Pushkin's Russian was largely confined to the language of educated people and conformed almost inevitably to the standards of elegance which the eighteenth century had sanctified . . . Of course, he made many inventions and greatly enriched the language of poetry, but he remains a classical poet in his finish, his neatness, his balance, his restraint.

The same point had been made earlier by Maurice Baring in his Introduction to the *Oxford Book of Russian Verse* (1925): "As to his form, his qualities as an artist can be summed up in one word, he is a classic. Classic in the same way that the Greeks are classic." Russian critics of Pushkin also share this view. Turgenev is by no means alone in speaking of Pushkin's "classical sense of proportion and harmony."

It is clear too that Pushkin himself was consciously guided by these classical stylistic canons. "True taste," he writes, for instance, in a note published in 1827, "consists not in the instinctive rejection of this or that word or turn of phrase but in a sense of proportion and appropriateness." And two years earlier we read in his unpublished essay "On Classical and Romantic Poetry": ". . . a difficulty overcome always brings us pleasure—that of loving the measure and harmony characteristic of the human intellect." "Precision and brevity" Pushkin considered "the most important qualities of prose," and in a draft note of 1826 the poet describes "calm" (which he contrasts with ecstasy) as "an absolute condition for beauty."

Associated with this predilection for cool simplicity, harmony, and elegance—this geometrical quality of mind—was a wonderfully light touch. More than any other writer in the history of Russian literature (Lermontov is perhaps his only rival), Pushkin possessed that facility of genius, the ability to make the most complex exercise appear easy. No better illustration of this supreme gift exists than *Eugene Onegin,* in which the intricately structured 14-line stanzas flow and dance with an apparently total ease and naturalness. In this, as in other respects, the comparison of Pushkin's poetry with the music of Mozart is still as valid as it is familiar. At the same time Pushkin was of course highly intelligent, in the sense of possessing an agile analytical brain, and the combination of this sharp mind with his sense of elegance and light touch inevitably found expression in those flashes of wit with which both his verse and his prose abound.

Pushkin's powers of observation, insight, and analysis are almost proverbial (indeed some of his lines have become proverbs), and this gift is reflected in that universal responsiveness and comprehension which have attracted comment from Russian critics. Had he been born thirty years later and been brought up in a different intellectual climate, Pushkin's talent for insight and analysis might have developed like Tolstoy's but, a true child of his age, Pushkin's response to the world was primarily an aesthetic one. The day when the artist would be a preacher, a rebel, or even a pervert had not yet arrived. Tomashevsky, arguing against the common tendency to "interpret"

Pushkin, explains in an essay that "for Pushkin himself every thought was to be judged as an artistic theme, from the point of view of its aesthetic potential." It was not literature's function, according to Pushkin, to serve moral or didactic ends. "The aim of poetry is poetry," he wrote to Zhukovsky in 1825 and repeated the same view in a review essay published six years later: "Poetry which by its higher and free nature should have no goal other than itself . . ." Critics too, Pushkin asserted, should be motivated, not by a variety of extraliterary considerations, but by a pure love of art and by the disinterested desire to discover the beauties and blemishes in works of literature. Even if a little evidence exists that toward the end of his life Pushkin was adopting a morally less neutral attitude toward literature, it still remains incontrovertible that his aesthetic sensibility remained, as always, far stronger than any moral impulse and that this quality, more than anything else, distinguishes him from the vast majority of Russian writers. "He possessed," opined Tolstoy in a conversation of 1900 recorded by A. Goldenweiser, "a more highly developed feeling for beauty than anyone else."

This amalgam of a classical sense of form, a light touch, a sparkling wit, and a highly developed aesthetic sense, which together with his self-confidence make Pushkin a truly aristocratic writer, also mark the poet off from the subsequent Russian nineteenth- and twentieth-century literary tradition. Pushkin—perhaps the last of the great European aristocratic poets—belongs to a past age in a way that Tolstoy and Dostoevsky, for instance, do not, and the further that age recedes into the past, the more difficult is the task of comprehending its spirit and the harder it becomes to appreciate Pushkin on his own terms.

In spite of all this, however, most literate Russians regard Pushkin as their national poet. This judgment often comes as a surprise to even the educated Western European who is likely to be far more familiar with the novels of Tolstoy and Dostoevsky or the plays of Chekhov than with any of Pushkin's works; indeed, he may well have come across the latter's name only in connection with Tchaikovsky's operas.

It is of course hard for foreigners to explain with any confidence what a poet means to his compatriots, but some attempt should be made to understand a little of what Russians appear to have in mind when they think of Pushkin, "Russia's first love," in the words of Tyutchev.

Pushkin's right to the title of Russia's national poet is justified perhaps primarily by his unique ability to evoke deep emotional responses from the Russian heart. For Russians, Pushkin is something very special, possessing qualities which, they feel, only a Russian can fully appreciate. As, for instance, an anonymous commentator quoted in *The Sunday Times* put it, "You English cannot know what Pushkin is for us. He is our pride, our hope and our love."

At the beginning of his essay on Pushkin, Alexander Blok emphasizes that the very name of Pushkin evokes pleasant sensations. In spite of the dark aspects which can be found in his work, Russians appear to associate Pushkin above all else with gaiety, sunshine, springtime, and childhood innocence; he evokes in them visions of a lost golden age when life was simpler and happier. Russians turn to him for confirmation of their hopes and for support in their sorrows, since he provides a joyful counter to both the harsh reality of Russian life and the Russian tendency to indulge in gloomy speculations. It is no coincidence that Pasternak's hero, Yuri Zhivago, for instance, sheltering in Varykino from the horrors of the Russian Revolution and Civil War, should attempt to renew his faith in life by constantly rereading Pushkin, whose optimism, openness, and almost childlike directness he contrasts with the morbid introspection of Gogol, Tolstoy, and Dostoevsky.

It is clear that Russian critics (and among them perhaps most notably Gogol, Belinsky, and Turgenev) tend to discuss Pushkin's status as the Russian national poet under two main headings: first, the poet's stature in comparison with the literary giants of other nations, and second, Pushkin's undisputed ability to express in his work what might be called the essence of the Russian national spirit.

Many Russian critics argue that Pushkin is the Russian equivalent of other acknowledged national poets,[2] such as Dante, Shakespeare, and Goethe. Like them, it is true, he assimilated previous literary traditions and achievements, added to these his own unique genius, and laid the foundations for subsequent literary developments in his homeland. He forged much of the modern Russian literary language, set an unsurpassed (indeed largely unemulated) aesthetic standard, and introduced a tone of universal sympathy. Numerous Russian men of letters—including writers as diverse in their style and spirit as Gogol and Turgenev, Tolstoy and Dostoevsky, or Bunin and Zamyatin—have testified to their indebtedness to Pushkin and their admiration for him. Turgenev even went so far as to proclaim that he would have sacrificed all his own works to have written a certain four of the poet's lines. Pushkin has clearly been an extraordinarily rich source of inspiration for his Russian literary successors, but it does not necessarily follow from this (as some Russian critics are wont to maintain) that without him there would have been, for instance, no Tolstoy and no Dostoevsky.

If Pushkin's stature *within* the Russian context cannot be disputed, it is by no means obvious that *outside* this context he possesses the same power to move the minds and hearts of men of other nations as do his supreme international rivals, or even as do the greatest of his Russian literary heirs. The argument that Pushkin loses more than they do in translation is not fully convincing: after all the highly individual poetry of Homer, Dante, Shakespeare, and Goethe survived even that ordeal. What Pushkin appears to lack in comparison with them is the weight and the obvious originality of the greatest minds. Interestingly enough, the more cosmopolitan of the Russian commentators, such as Turgenev, Solovyov, or Mirsky, for example, tend to be less pretentious in their assertions about Pushkin's international status. And indeed a claim like Stepanov's that *"The Captain's Daughter* occupies a prime position in world literature," by distracting attention from Pushkin's individual Russian genius, may do the poet more of a disservice than Mirsky's superficially harsh judgment that "on the scale of world history Pushkin does not mark a new step forward."

For the majority of Russians, however—critics and ordinary readers alike—the necessarily inconclusive debate about Pushkin's achievements in comparison with those of Shakespeare or Goethe is largely irrelevant. For them Pushkin is "the father of Russian literature," "the founder of the Russian literary language," and, most important, the writer who, apart from possessing a captivating aura of gaiety and innocence, embodies for Russians the essence of their national spirit.

Gogol's assessment of Pushkin as the Russian national poet in this sense of the term has rarely been disputed:

> The countryside, soul, language and character of Russia are reflected in him with the purity and the spotless perfection with which a landscape is reflected through the convex surface of a lens . . . From the very first he was a national poet because the true expression of national spirit rests not in the description of peasant costume, but in the very spirit of the people.

In spite of the strong French influence to which he was subjected in his upbringing—or perhaps that influence paradoxically provided a firm platform and an appropriate perspective from which he could observe Russia—Pushkin heard the Russian language and saw Russian life with an unprecedented and unsurpassed clarity.

Of course the time was ripe for this achievement. At the beginning of the nineteenth century the belated development of a Russian national consciousness was starting to gather pace. A growing national pride which had been boosted by Russia's role in the defeat of Napoleon coincided with the fashionable predilection of the European Romantic movement for examining each nation's historical roots and cultural heritage. Born at the very end of the eighteenth century, Pushkin was both a product of this new national spirit in Russia and a leading contributor to it in the field of literature.

Russian eighteenth-century literature could boast of little that was purely Russian: like the rest of Russian aristocratic culture, it limped behind European fashions, aping European genres, conventions, poses, and idioms. With Pushkin, Russian literature suddenly found a new life. "In his verses," wrote Dobrolyubov, "we heard for the first time the living Russian language and saw for the first time our authentic Russian world."

Like a new Adam, Pushkin looked upon Russian life with a penetrating and apparently innocent eye and described his visions with a freshness and vigor which still charm today. Many of his depictions and insights became *topoi,* not only for subsequent Russian writers, but for countless ordinary readers, who find their own experiences in Pushkin and see the world through Pushkinian spectacles. A vivid account of this process is provided in Bunin's novel *Arsenev's Life.* In a chapter devoted to describing the impact of Pushkin on his youthful imagination, the semi-autobiographical narrator cites various verses from the poet which struck deep chords within him and emphasizes the intimate correspondence between his own reactions and Pushkin's lines: "How many emotions he evoked in me! And how often my own emotions and everything amidst which and by which I lived found a companion in him!"

Russian readers of Pushkin are struck by both the range and the depth of the poet's understanding of Russian life. In a famous judgment for which Pisarev took him to task, Belinsky described *Eugene Onegin* as "an encyclopedia of Russian life." Pisarev is right when he points out that Pushkin almost completely ignores the political and economic realities of the day, the vital concerns of the peasantry and the growing urban middle class, and the many serious intellectual debates conducted during the period the work describes, but in spite of this Belinsky's remark is far from absurd: the poet's novel in verse provides an astonishingly full gallery of contemporary portraits, interiors, and landscapes, a lively account of numerous Russian habits, customs, and beliefs, and an accurate record of the way many ordinary Russians of the day lived and thought. More important than this documentary quality of *Eugene Onegin,* however, is of course Pushkin's magical facility for discerning in Russian life and embodying in a brilliant literary form those features which strike fellow Russians (his readers) as both quintessentially typical and touchingly poetic.

The same facility informs not only Pushkin's other works set in contemporary Russia (including his lyrics) but also the works he set in historical times, whether in dramatic form *(Boris Godunov),* in verse *(The Bronze Horseman),* or in prose *(The Captain's Daughter).* Here the poet re-creates, in a wholly convincing way for Russians, not merely the events but, more profoundly, the underlying essence and the enduring spirit of the Russian past.

Pushkin's appreciation of the Russian national spirit is for Russians further demonstrated by the poet's feeling for the Russian folk tradition, elements from which figure prominently *inter alia* in the early *Ruslan and Lyudmila* and the later fairy tales in verse.

In discussions of the latter (as, for example, in Slonimsky's essay) Russian critics usually refer to the poet's nanny Arina Rodionovna, from whom much of the poet's knowledge of Russian folklore is said to derive and who, more generally, provided the boy Pushkin with his first insights into the nature of the ordinary uneducated Russians who formed the vast bulk of the country's population. Soviet critics, who for political reasons must exaggerate Pushkin's alleged sympathies with the "broad masses," have naturally given particular prominence to Arina Rodionovna's role in the poet's development—sometimes to the extent that she has seemed to bear on her frail shoulders almost the entire weight of Pushkin's Russianness.

The subject matter, settings, and inspiration of Pushkin's works are, however, clearly not exclusively Russian: indeed, in his creative sympathies the poet ranges so widely that some Russian critics extol primarily his universal responsiveness, his ability to comprehend and re-create the atmosphere and spirit of other peoples, present and past. Critics who recognize and value this gift but also want to preserve their image of Pushkin as an incarnation of the Russian national spirit are then driven to the curious and highly dubious argument propounded most passionately by Dostoevsky. This argument—a plain assertion that a single exceptional case is also typical—maintains that precisely a spirit of universality is the uniquely Russian virtue and achievement; in other words, Pushkin, we have to believe, in both his obvious Russianness and in his obvious non-Russianness is being equally Russian!

Pushkin's own opinions of his Russian homeland, like his literary roots and inspirations, were characteristically complex. On the one hand he seemed to feel an almost maternal affection for his country's language, its culture, its history, and its destiny, but on the other he could write of his utter contempt, as in his letter to Vyazemsky of May 1826:

> Of course I despise my country from head to toe, but I am irritated when a foreigner shares my view. How can you, who are free to go wherever you like, stay in Russia? If the Tsar grants me *freedom,* I won't stay a month. We live in miserable times, but when I imagine London, railways, steamships, English journals or the theaters and brothels of Paris, my remote Mikhailovskoye induces in me a sense of melancholy and rage.

Pushkin's relationship with the Tsar and his attitude to the institution of autocracy were ambivalent and he expressed at various times during his comparatively short life liberal (if not revolutionary) and conservative (not to say reactionary) views. But Pushkin was not really a political animal; he was above all and *par excellence* an artist and it is to his art rather than his politics that attention must be directed.

The central paradox of Pushkin's art remains the unique and

remarkable relationship between its form and its content: even those works which strike his compatriots as quintessentially Russian are couched in a style which, perhaps French in inspiration, is markedly un-Russian in its formal elegance. It might seem hardly unfair to claim that Pushkin's works are Russian *in spite of* their form, or that, conversely, they are un-Russian *in spite of* their content; and indeed at least tacit support can be given to such a formulation both by those many critics who discuss the subject matter of Pushkin's works without reference to their form and by those (far rarer in Russia) who analyze the poet's formal structures and devices while ignoring his content. Pushkin's supreme artistic achievement, however, must be seen to be his masterly integration of these two disparate elements to create a wondrous higher harmony and unity. It is a harmony and unity which make Pushkin's work neither Russian nor (let us say) French, but something greater than both, and in responding to his work, the reader is moved not only by its Russianness or its Frenchness, not only by its content or its form, taken separately, not only by any individual component elements (intellect or emotion, wit or worship, purity or ribaldry), but above all by that all-embracing aesthetic balance of great classical art which soothes and uplifts because it reminds man of his lost hopes and ideals and provides an earnest of their possible realization.

Gogol's celebrated remark that Pushkin "represents a stage to which Russians will have developed in perhaps 200 years' time" is now annoying in its narrow chauvinism and poignant in its naïveté: Pushkin's work represents universal aesthetic ideals, but ideals whose fulfillment is in the modern world becoming ever less likely. On the other hand, as these ideals of harmony and elegance lose their former power over the minds of men, those who still value them turn with greater love and gratitude to Pushkin.

NOTES

1. In his book on Pushkin written while he was in England in the 1920's, Mirsky suggests that "on the whole the French have failed to appreciate Pushkin's work, probably for the very reason that he excelled them in all the qualities which they regard as peculiarly their own"!

2. Debates conducted in Russian about Pushkin's status as a national poet are apt to become complex, if not confused, because of the semantic range of the two Russian adjectives *natsional'nyi* and *narodnyi*. The latter in particular creates problems of comprehension (and translation) because in various contexts it refers to at least three distinct but overlapping concepts: (1) the nation as a symbolic entity; (2) the population of the nation as a whole; or (3) the simple working masses, or "folk."

Marginal Notes on Eugene Onegin [1]

ROMAN JAKOBSON

"The Crimea is the cradle of my Onegin," [2] wrote Pushkin shortly before his death. The poet considered the Caucasian and Crimean trip that he took in 1820 with the Rayevsky family the happiest moment of his life. Reminiscences of Pushkin's secret but unforgotten Crimean love, Maria Rayevskaya, have been traced in his novel and not only in its lyrical passages but also in several of Tatyana Larina's features. In 1825, shortly before the Decembrists' rebellion, Maria Rayevskaya had married Prince Volkonsky, a man twenty years her elder, and she had heroically followed him to a Siberian prison to which he had been sentenced for his participation in this rebellion. Literary historians have also found correspondences between Eugene Onegin and Alexander Rayevsky, Maria's brother and the famous model for Pushkin's "Demon," a lyric poem of 1823. It was at the Rayevskys' in the Crimea that Pushkin became acquainted with the works of Lord Byron, whose influence fades and is overcome in *Onegin*. Pushkin takes the characteristic strophic construction of *Eugene Onegin* and a whole strophe for its first chapter, on which he began work in May of the following year at Kishinyov, from his own sketches for *Taurida* (dated 1822), an unrealized lyric novel on the Crimean theme.

He admits that he is satisfied with the beginning of the new poem, which, he says, seldom happens to him. He persuasively insists that it is his best work. When the first chapters gradually appear, they meet with singular success. "They are the general topic of conversation," reports the *Moskovsky Vestnik* [Moscow Messenger] in 1828, "women and girls, men of letters and men about town ask one another upon meeting: Do you know *Onegin?* How do you like the new cantos? What do you say about Tanya? About Olga? About Lensky? etc." Likewise a bulletin of 1840 announces: "They are reading it in every nook and corner of the Russian Empire, in all the strata of Russian society, and everyone knows several couplets by heart. Many of the poet's thoughts have become proverbs." Leading Russian critics found *Onegin* Pushkin's most original book, and the renowned Belinsky said: "To evaluate such a work means to evaluate the poet himself in the whole range of his creative activity." 3 Both the praise and the negation of Pushkin's legacy have rested primarily on *Onegin.* And even if *Onegin* sometimes makes more of a historical, museum-like impression upon the literary epoch which began with the Symbolists than, for example, the ever more contemporary *Bronze Horseman* or *Queen of Spades,* the assertion of one of Pushkin's contemporaries is nevertheless still valid 110 years later: "Everyone is fascinated by Tatyana's dream—lovers of delirium, lovers of reality, and lovers of poetry." In this stifling and portentous dream, which Pushkin created in the days when terror was oppressing the vanquished Decembrists, the reality of delirium becomes visionary poetry that suddenly brings the whole image of the impassioned Tatyana incredibly close to lyricism of today, and the arid sketch of her ghostly visions comes incredibly close to a modern, unrestrained grotesque of paranoiac tint.

In March 1824 Pushkin informed a friend from his place of exile in Odessa: "I am writing the variegated stanzas of a Romantic epic and am taking lessons in pure atheism." 4 This epic or "novel in verse" is *Eugene Onegin.* What ties it to Romanticism? Modern literary-historical research rightly emphasizes that the motive force of this work is *Romantic irony,* which presents the same thing from conflicting points of view, now as grotesque, now as serious, now as simultaneously grotesque and serious. This irony is the distinctive feature of the hopelessly skeptical hero, but it outgrows its characterizing function and, in fact, colors the entire plot of the novel, as if it were being seen through the hero's eyes. A contemporaneous reviewer appropriately compared *Onegin* to a musical capriccio and grasped that "the poet is constantly playing, now with a thought, now with an emotion, now with imagination; he is alternately gay and pensive, frivolous and profound, derisive and sentimental, spiteful and good-natured; he doesn't let a single one of our mental faculties slumber, but he doesn't hold onto any one and he doesn't satisfy any one." The cancellation of a fixed order of values, the constant interpenetration of elevated and lowly, even derisive, shots of the same object obliterates the boundary between the solemn and the ordinary, between the tragic and the comic. What is present here is the supreme art of *proprie communia dicere,* which is what Mérimée and Turgenev admired in Pushkin, and at the same time there is the art of saying the most complex things simply, which is the feature of *Onegin* that captivated the subtlest of the Russian Romantics, Baratynsky. Pushkin's linguistic devices produced the impression of words that were accidental, natural, casual and at the same time supremely deliberate, disciplined, and close-fitting.

As Belinsky rightly pointed out, negation resembles admiration in the poet's novel. Thus despite a crushing image of Russian society—whether that of the city or that of the country—in Pushkin's novel, critics who saw in it a welcome counterbalance to a satirically pointed literature (Druzhinin) were not mistaken. Indeed, even the poet himself gives contradictory answers to the question whether there is satire in *Onegin*. The elegiac stanzas on Lensky's demise are altered by the suggestion of another possibility—by a tentative happy ending, by the negation of a senseless death, by a vision of that glorious future which perhaps awaited the youthful poet; however, the opposite possibility—Lensky's gradual spiritual decay—is outlined immediately thereafter. The reverent pathos of the preceding image is canceled, and the youth's tragic death acquires a certain justification. Eugene's supreme drama—his amorous infatuation with Tatyana—is presented on two levels, one tragic and the other farcical, while the action of the novel is confined to the comic situation of a suitor surprised by his love's husband. The action concludes, but the novel ends only with the evocation of the two leading lyrical motifs of the whole work. These are, on the one hand, the ideal image of Tanya and, in the distance, a shade of the poet's reminiscences, which from time to time flicker behind her and, on the other hand, the theme of vanishing youth, which is always irretrievable and which rejects every substitute as blasphemy. This theme pervades the entire novel, and the wise Herzen shrewdly perceived that Onegin kills the ideal of his own youth in Lensky and that the aging Onegin's love for Tatyana is only a last tragic dream of irretrievable youth. The image of youth and the image of Tanya create a thread of pure lyricism in Pushkin's novel.

The verse structure purposely calls attention to the poet-narrator: "I am now writing not a novel but a novel in verse—the devil of a difference,"[5] discloses Pushkin. Both the author and the reader, as well as the true participants in the action, are constant, active characters in *Eugene Onegin*. Their points of view are intertwined in various ways, and the interpenetration of subjective meanings creates the impression of the supra-personal, Olympian objectivity of the work. Internal discrepancies are a conscious component of the work, as Pushkin acknowledges in accord with Romantic poetics; a certain oscillation of meaning must be allowed. Too much definitiveness would have mortified the growth of the poem; on the contrary, the impression of the vague range of a *free,* unplanned novel had to be strengthened. The original preface to the first chapter professed doubt as to whether the poem would ever be finished.

According to his own calculation Pushkin worked on *Onegin* for seven years, four months, and seventeen days (May 9, 1823, to September 25, 1830); the final revision of the last chapter took another year. During this period many events took place in the lives of Pushkin and his friends, of the Russian Empire and Europe. His position and outlook changed substantially. His conception of the novel and his relation to his heroes also changed; the plot crystallized in new ways and took new directions. The poet's age increased along with Onegin's chapters about squandered, vanishing youth. The course of his life became the dynamics of his work; the change in the writer's views on life caused inconsistencies between separate sections of the novel and enhanced its vitality. The alternation of different points of view on one and the same thing perfectly accords with Pushkin's poetics, and thus Belinsky's shrewd paradox proves to be true: the very defects of *Eugene Onegin* constitute its great asset.

Each of Pushkin's images is so elastically polysemantic and manifests such an amazing assimilatory capacity that it easily fits into the most varied contexts. Pushkin's renowned power of poetic transformation is also related to this fact. Hence the features of *Onegin*'s author are different beyond recognition for diverse critics. In his famous invectives against *Onegin* Pisarev maintains that Belinsky loved a Pushkin whom he himself had created, but it may be said with equal justification that Pisarev hated a Pushkin of his own fabrication, and the same may be repeated *mutatis mutandis* about every attempt at a unilateral interpretation of Pushkin's work. If we realize, as did the attentive Dobrolyubov, that Pushkin did not introduce a unifying sense into his images, we shall comprehend the futility of the endless arguments about how to interpret the multiplicity of meanings of his novel epistemologically—as a wealth of content or as a lack of content—and how to evaluate it ethically—as a moral lesson or as a profession of amorality. We shall comprehend how it is possible that *Eugene Onegin* is a manifestation of powerless despair for one outstanding author and an expression of profound epicureanism for another and how it is possible that such contradictory judgments about the title hero as Belinsky's eulogy and Pisarev's censure can occur. Tatyana's meditation on Onegin in stanza 24 of the seventh chapter with its chain of contradictory, doubting questions is a telling example of Pushkin's oscillating characterizations. A similar bifurcation, which is, however, motivated developmentally ("Uzhel' ta samaya Tat'yana

. . . Kak izmenilasya Tat'yana!"),[6] distinguishes the characterization of Tatyana in the last chapter.

Either this kind of *oscillating characterization* evokes the notion of a unique, complex, unrepeatable individuality or, if the reader is accustomed to clear-cut typification, he gets the impression (let us cite several notable expressions of Pushkin's time) that in the novel "characters are lacking," "the hero is only a connecting link of descriptions," "the characterizations are pale," "Onegin is not depicted profoundly; Tatyana does not have typical traits," etc. Later attempts by different commentators to perceive Onegin as a type either attained results that quite comically contradicted one another or produced such paradoxical formulae as "a typical exception." It is precisely the premise that Onegin is primarily a historical type that leads to a common error, which even the famous historian Klyuchevsky has repeated after Herzen in a special essay: Oneginism has to be the result of the unsuccessful December rebellion of 1825; Onegin, they say, is a defeated Decembrist. Literary-historical scholarship has shown, however, that according to the minute data of the novel its action occurs in the first half of the twenties and its conclusion in the spring of 1825. Moreover, two-thirds of *Onegin* had been written prior to the end of that year. As Ryleyev's and Bestuzhev's letters to Pushkin eloquently attest, Eugene's general defeatism was entirely unacceptable and equally inopportune for the future Decembrists, just as were his icy preaching to the enamored Tanya and his profession of love to the "indifferent princess," and, actually—here Herzen is right,—as was Onegin's entire existence.

Attempts at an unambiguous appraisal of the social tendency of the novel have also been unsuccessful. Pushkin begins Onegin under the sign of impetuous rebellion. He informs his friends of this in conspiratorial terms (in case of police inspection of correspondence). He writes that he is choking on bile and that "if the poem is ever printed, it will certainly not happen either in Moscow or in St. Petersburg."[7] From the beginning a mood of despair, which, owing to the mounting reaction at home and the defeats of the revolutionary movement in Europe, overcomes the Bessarabian exile, is associated with the rebellion. It is reflected most vigorously in Pushkin's lyric poetry of that period. The despair mounts, the poet gradually conforms to the censorship, his rebellion is more and more concealed. Finally, even an unobjectionable sentence often becomes a tragic allusion in light of the ominous events around December 1825. In the last stanza of the novel a citation from Saadi, which not long ago had seemed to be innocently ornamental, "Inykh uzh net, a te daleche," 8 becomes a reminiscence of the executed and imprisoned Decembrists, and Lensky's death is associated with the imprisonment of his model, Küchelbecker. The theme of resignation intensifies with each chapter and culminates in Tatyana's final words: "No ya drugomu otdana;/Ya budu vek yemu verna." 9 In his renowned speech on Pushkin, Dostoevsky —in opposition to Belinsky—finds in these words not a tragedy of resignation before life but an apotheosis of resignation, and he attempts to ground it esthetically and to extend it to Pushkin's entire work. But Tatyana's thesis also recurs shortly after the concluding chapter of *Onegin* (completed at the end of September 1830) in the poet's prose—in *The Blizzard* (October 1830) and in *Dubrovsky* (1832–33)—as a naked expression of resignation, and here it is not possible to apply Dostoevsky's interpretation ethically. Moreover, this motif is entirely alien to the work of Pushkin's youth: it is directly ridiculed in *Count Nulin* (1825), and in *The Gypsies* (1823–24), to which Dostoevsky refers, it is precisely the one seeking that eternal fidelity who is harshly condemned.

If the author of *The Possessed* wanted to ascribe to Pushkin's work a resolute warning against a "fantastic" revolutionary action, the antipode of Dostoevsky, Pisarev is also disposed, in his polemics with Belinsky, to detect the same tendency: "The whole *Eugene Onegin* is nothing but a colorful and flashy apotheosis of the most hopeless and senseless status quo." 10 The recently decoded fragments of a further chapter of the novel patently reveal the erroneousness of this biased, one-sided interpretation. This chapter, a compact survey of the Russian and European revolutionary struggle against reaction, satisfied the poet's inner need: there could not have been any thought of publishing such an openly incendiary and antitsaristic reflection; indeed, even the circulation of the manuscript would have threatened the poet with severe punishment. In October 1830 he burned it for fear of a search of his house, and he kept only an encoded record of the beginnings of several stanzas:

> Vlastitel' slabyi i lukavyi,
> Pleshivyi shchëgol', vrag truda,
> Nechayanno prigretyi slavoy,
> Nad nami tsarstvoval togda, etc.11

The Decembrists' rebellion was apparently to have been the kernel of the chapter; the action of the preceding chapter ends just several months before the rebellion. What kind of role was Eugene to play in it? Was Princess Maria Volkonskaya's heroic part to fall to Princess Tatyana? Here we can actually apply Dostoevsky's famous words about the great mystery that Pushkin took to his grave and that we are now solving without him.

NOTES

1. Translated from the Czech original, "Na okraj Eugena One-gina," *Vybrané spisy A. S. Puškina* II, ed. A. Bém and R. Jakobson (Prague, 1937), pp. 257–64.

2. "C'est le berceau de mon 'Onegin . . .'" (Letter of November 10, 1836, to N. B. Golitsyn; *Polnoye Sobraniye Sochineniy* X, 602).

3. V. G. Belinsky, *Sochineniya Aleksandra Pushkina*, ed. N. I. Mordovchenko (Leningrad, 1937), p. 385.

4. ". . . pishu pestrye strofy romanticheskoy poemy—i beru uroki chistogo afeizma . . ." (Letter of March 1824, to P. A. Vyazemsky [?]; N. V. Bogoslovsky, ed., *Pushkin o literature* [Moscow-Leningrad: Academy, 1934], p. 46).

5. ". . . ya teper' pishu ne roman, a roman v stikhakh—dyavol'-skaya raznitsa" (Letter of November 4, 1823, to P. A. Vyazemsky; *PSS* X, 70).

6. ["Is it really the same Tatyana (20) . . . How Tatyana has changed" (28)].

7. ". . . esli kogda-nibud' ona i budet napechatana, to verno ne v Moskve i ne v Peterburge" (Letter of February 8, 1824, to A. A. Bestuzhev; *PSS* X, 82).

8. ["Some are already no more, and the other ones are far away."] Earlier Pushkin had used this citation from Saadi as the epigraph for *The Fountain of Bakhchisaray.*

9. ["But I am given in wedlock to another, and I will be faithful to him forever."] It is precisely this motif of hopeless resignation that Pushkin directly links in "Onegin's Journey" with his avowal of retreat from romanticism, which some Soviet critics through a peculiar misunderstanding take to be a revolutionary element in the poet's development.

10. D. I. Pisarev, "Pushkin i Belinsky" (1865), *Polnoye Sobraniye Sochineniy,* 6 vols. (4th ed.; St. Petersburg, 1904), V, p. 63.

11. ["A weak and insidious ruler, a bald-headed fop, a foe of work, unexpectedly warmed by glory, reigned over us at that time"] (*PSS* V, 209).

The Author-Narrator's Stance in Onegin

J. THOMAS SHAW

I

William Faulkner, in the foreword to *The Mansion,* the "final chapter" of his Snopes family trilogy, acknowledged that there are "discrepancies and contradictions" in the multivolume work, which was written and published over a large number of years. It was written from 1925 to 1959, published from 1940 to 1959; and its main fictional action extends from about 1916 to 1946. Faulkner attributed the "discrepancies and contradictions" to the "fact that the author has learned, he believes, more about the human heart than he knew [when he began it] thirty-four years ago, and is sure that, having lived with them that long, he knows the characters in the chronicle better than he did then."

Thus Faulkner attributed the "discrepancies and contradictions" in the trilogy to his own growth and development during the long period when he was writing these three novels. He could have pointed out that within the trilogy the characters also grow and develop in a fictional world which reflects the real world, not only of the region, but of the nation and the globe—including World War I, the Depression of the 1930's, and World War II and its immediate aftermath. One may well ask what unity or consistency of stance behind such a multivolume work can there be to allow for the author's development, and for his own and his characters' reactions to large changes in the real world after he began writing, and then after he began publishing it. In Faulkner's trilogy, there is overlapping time of writing, of publication, and of the fictional action. I leave to Faulkner specialists the question of the unity of the author's basic stance behind the trilogy and what difference this may make for understanding and appreciating it.

In almost every way, one would think, Pushkin's novel in verse is a work poles apart from Faulkner's prose trilogy. Nevertheless, *Onegin* presents a number of complexities for interpretation and evaluation comparable to those we have just noted for Faulkner's trilogy. Here we shall focus on only one: the search for the unity of stance behind the work which accommodates the author's development and reactions to the real world after he began writing and publishing—in sections and at intervals over a whole decade before it all appeared in one binding—a work which likewise has overlapping times of writing, of publishing, and of fictional action, and in which the characters and the author develop while the novel is being written and published. The time spans are much smaller than in Faulkner's trilogy, but the years comprise a period of crisis for Pushkin and for Russia.

Faulkner's trilogy uses the third-person, omniscient-author technique, so that any "discrepancies and contradictions" in the implied author behind the omniscient narrator are largely concealed. Pushkin's novel in verse is narrated in the first person by a poetic representative of Pushkin himself—who not only has written Pushkin's poetry, which it is assumed the reader of this novel knows, but also has had Pushkin's relevant life experiences, which it is assumed the reader of the novel also knows. Furthermore, the author-narrator is made a character in the fictional action: briefly, in the first chapter, as a friend of Onegin's in St. Petersburg before Onegin and he go their separate ways. This author-narrator allows himself the astonishing expanse of almost one-third of the space of the entire novel for "digressions" on themes suggested by the main action. These digressions offer showers of apparent "discrepancies and contradictions." They are in a multitude of tones, from matter-of-fact comment to intense lyricism, and with many levels of irony, often apparently contradictory, from the effervescent playful to the mordant. In the massive scholarship and criticism on *Onegin* the question of the consistency of the author's stance has been almost completely ignored. Insofar as an opinion on this subject has even been suggested, the implication seems to have been that such unity of stance may be lacking. This essay will argue that there is unity of stance behind the author-narrator and attempt to determine its nature.

The time of the fictional action in *Onegin* extends from winter/spring 1819/20 to spring 1825. It is important enough to the author that he made it determinable within the work. The first of these dates was supplied in the preface to the first chapter, and the further events in the novel can be dated by indications in it of the passing of time. The individual chapters of the novel were published as separate small volumes from February 1825 to 1832, before the entire work appeared in one binding in 1833. The first chapter appeared as a separate book about two months before the end of the fictional action of the entire work. In publishing each of the first two chapters, Pushkin made a point of indicating clearly the year of composition as 1823, thereby suggesting that as the time of narration of those chapters.

Tone, phrasing, and internal evidence also indicate that the reader is meant to consider the time of narration of the remaining chapters the same as the time of writing. Thus there is an implied continual development of the author during the writing of the novel proper, from 1823 to 1830. In addition, when the author-narrator presents himself in the first chapter as a character, it is his self of 1819/20 that he presents. Thus the time of narration is 1823 to 1830, and the narrator presents himself, additionally, as a character "as of" 1819/20.

One function served by the use of the author-narrator as a character in the first chapter is to present him at the earlier

moment and to imply that there may be significant development in him between 1820 and the time of writing the first
chapter, 1823.

The time of the fictional action of the novel, 1820 to 1825, all
falls within the reign of Alexander I. The time of narration
(the same as the time of writing) includes the last two years
of Alexander I's reign, and extends some five years into the
reign of Nicholas I. The span of narration time in the novel
implies the narrator's reacting to the events of the real world,
including, among others, the Decembrist uprising (December
1825), six months after the end of the fictional action of the
novel and five years before the end of the time of narration.
Political events never become explicit themes in *Onegin;* the
censor would not have allowed it, even if Pushkin had wished
it. Nevertheless, the narrator's present-tense consciousness always
implies awareness of personal, social, and political life up to the
time of writing each of the individual chapters in turn.

The time spans of *Onegin* mark a time of crises—or at any
rate, great changes—not only in Pushkin's way of looking
at the world but also in his mode of writing. The author-
narrator presented as a character in Chapter I is a representation
of Pushkin on the eve of being exiled for "subversive" (liberal;
Russians usually say "revolutionary") poems. Half the novel
(the first four chapters) was written during Alexander I's
reign. Readers of the first two chapters were made aware, as we
have seen, that they were written in 1823 while Pushkin was
in exile. Pushkin continued in exile while the next two chapters
(III and IV) were being written in 1824–1825, and up to the
time of Nicholas I's coronation in August 1826. Between December 1825 (the time of the Decembrist uprising) and Nicholas
I's coronation, Pushkin wrote Chapters V and VI. The final
two chapters were written from 1827 to 1830, except for one
inserted "document," Onegin's letter, which was written in the
fall of 1831. Thus the narrational time of the novel's final chapters implies the narrator's living under Nicholas I.

It is not surprising that in a country where, under the

strict censorship, the use of "Aesopic language" has long been the way for concealing or revealing true intent in literary works, there have been continuing attempts to read between the lines—and past the end—of the novel, to interpret its words, characters, and story as containing concealed allusions and implied attitudes toward what could not be openly discussed —such as the reigns of Alexander I and Nicholas I and the Decembrist uprising and its aftermath. Half the novel had been written and one chapter published before December 1825. It can hardly be overemphasized that Pushkin not only managed to continue and complete the novel but also to include in the total work without any basic subsequent revisions all the chapters he wrote while he was in exile.

Pushkin is always a craftsman, a builder of harmonious literary structures, including the "free novel," as he called *Onegin*. It is always dangerous to assume that he did not know what he was doing. By completing *Onegin* as he began it, without basic revision of the early parts, he showed that to his artistic consciousness there is adequate unity and conformity in the total novel in all aspects, including the basic author-narrator's stance. Thus the question is not whether there is basic unity of the author-narrator's stance, but what is the nature of that stance? Perhaps the best way to approach characterizing that stance is through a little lyric poem he wrote in 1823, during the early stages of his work on *Onegin*.

2

Pushkin interrupted writing the early part of *Onegin* to write "The Demon," a lyric which was obviously closely connected in his consciousness with his novel in verse. Indeed, he wrote the only surviving manuscript draft of it on a manuscript page of the first chapter of *Onegin* and he refers to it specifically in the last chapter of the novel (written seven years later). The lyric is short enough to be quoted here: I shall give it in prose translation. The poem, as written, has two parts. The first is as follows:

> In the days when all the impressions of
> existence were new to me—the glances of
> maidens, the rustle of a grove, and the
> singing of a nightingale at night; when sublime
> feelings—freedom, glory, and love—and the inspired
> arts were agitating my blood so strongly. . . .

It will be noted that this passage presents and brings to a close a whole stage of "existence": the poem expresses, in the author-persona's first person, the young poet's ability to perceive freshly and directly: beauty of appearance (girls' "glances" —that is, eyes; and, metonymically, all feminine beauty), of sound (rustle of trees, singing of nightingales), and "sublime feelings"—freedom, glory, love. All these impressions and feelings provide inspiration for the poet. To this point, poetry has been the poetry of perception, and in this sense youth may be "poetic."

The second part of the poem, continuing the same sentence, describes what brought that stage to an end and replaced it:

> Then, casting a shadow of sudden anguish,
> a certain malicious genius began to visit
> me in secret. Our meetings were sad:
> his smile, his wondrous glance, his
> wounding speeches poured cold venom
> into my soul. With inexhaustible
> slander he would tempt providence;
> he called the beautiful a dream;
> he contemned inspiration; he disbelieved
> in love, in freedom; he looked on life
> scornfully, and nothing in all nature
> was he inclined to bless.

In this second stage, a supernatural being is presented as visiting the youthful poet and casting "venom" on what he had experienced and prized: beauty of sight and sound; inspiration, love, freedom. The demon "blesses," that is, accepts, nothing in all "nature," that is, existence. Thus the negative figure disparages all the experiences of the poet-youth's first stage. The implication is clear that the demon infected the youthful poet with his own attitude, so that to the young poet his coming represents the coming of a second stage—disenchantment with all that had previously enchanted him. Here the poem, as written, stops.

To this day, this lyric has been interpreted as one of disenchantment, as presenting the poet-persona (identified as Pushkin himself) as still in the stage of disenchantment. This interpretation suggests that Pushkin overcame the spiritual crisis of disenchantment only later; just when has long been the subject of disagreement among Pushkin specialists. I suggest that this interpretation presents an inadequate understanding of the poem. Lyric poems are in the present tense of the author-persona's perception of the state or experience presented in them. However, this poem as we have it is totally in the past tense. Hence the present tense of the poem, the present-tense mood behind the poem, is implicit rather than stated. What is this present-tense attitude?

Among the things the demon conveyed to the impressionable young poet was scorn of inspiration. However, the existence of the poem shows that if the demon's "visits" resulted in the loss of inspiration, such loss of inspiration was only temporary. If inspiration ceased, it has resumed, using as its subject the presence and then the absence of what induced inspiration. This inspiration sees through the negation, doubt, disenchantment of the second stage to the positive qualities of the first stage (youthful impressionability, perceptivity, inspiration) and presents them vitally in the experience of the poem, so that the result is re-enchantment with that experience and those qualities. This reenchantment does not, however, deny the reality or even the value of the experience of doubt and questioning; indeed, it suggests that the values of youthful enchantment are revalued after that experience. (Youth is too precious to waste on the

young.) So that the "feelings" the demon has cast venom upon
are restored in value in spite of and also through their being
questioned.

Thus the poem, properly understood, implies a third stage.
After the first stage of youthful enchantment comes a second
stage of disenchantment with all that had earlier been enchanting, and this second stage is followed by an implied stage of
mature reenchantment, the implied present tense of the poem.
This third stage is one of sophisticated naïveté, or ingenuous
sophistication. This third stage marks the climax and culmina-
tion of the poem, and represents the stance of the author-
persona of the poem. This stance is one that will permit further
maturing, with whatever experiences that may bring.

3

Nobody has ever doubted that the author-persona of "The
Demon" is to be interpreted as being a poetic representation—
however stylized—of Pushkin himself. Neither has anyone ever
doubted that the first-person author-narrator of *Onegin* is to
be interpreted as a poetic representation—however stylized—of
Pushkin: as one who has written Pushkin's previous poetry
and lived Pushkin's relevant life experiences. A question that
has not been faced hitherto is the unity and nature of the author-
narrator's stance in *Onegin*. Neither has the related question
been adequately answered: the function served by "Pushkin"
as author-narrator presenting "himself" briefly as a character in
Chapter I of the novel.

It is my thesis that from the beginning of Chapter I of
Onegin the author-narrator's stance in it is basically what I have
just interpreted as the author-persona's implied present-tense
stance in the lyric "The Demon": that of one who has gone
through a stage of youthful perceptivity and enchantment,
followed by a stage of disenchantment, followed by a third stage
(the implied present tense of narrating the novel) of mature reenchantment. In speaking in the first person as author-narrator

and in making "himself" briefly a character in the novel, Pushkin builds on the expectation that readers of *Onegin* will be aware of his earlier published works and even of such a major event in his personal life as his removal from St. Petersburg and the reason for it.

It cannot be an accident that Pushkin made it explicit that the fictional time of Chapter I is 1819/20, but the time of writing is 1823, and the place of writing is Kishinyov and then Odessa. Thus the time of narrating Chapter I, and hence of the author-narrator's stance in it, is made definite as being 1823. The author-narrator's friendship with the fictional Onegin, in 1819/20, was on the eve of Onegin's departure to his uncle's country estate, where the main fictional action of the novel begins, and on the eve of Pushkin's exile to South Russia for writing his early "subversive" ("revolutionary") poems. Thus Pushkin made certain that his readers could see that Chapter I presents the way the poet-Pushkin in 1823 looked upon himself as having been in 1820.

Pushkin's readers were aware that in 1820, and before, Pushkin had written poetry having the qualities of what we have called the first stage of "The Demon," poetry expressing the young poet's ability to perceive freshly and directly: beauty of appearance, of sound, and "elevated feelings" of freedom, glory, love. The readers of *Onegin* also knew that between 1820 and 1823 Pushkin had written and published lyrics with a disenchanted author-persona, and a long narrative poem, *The Prisoner of the Caucasus,* which has a disenchanted hero with whom, as Pushkin acknowledged, there is an essential identification of hero's and implied author's stance. In short, readers of *Onegin* were aware that Pushkin had experienced, in succession, the two explicit stages of "The Demon." In the passage in Chapter I, where the author-narrator is presented as having been in friendly personal relationships with his hero Onegin in 1820, Pushkin makes it explicit that there is not such an identification of disenchanted hero and the author-narrator in this novel. So that the chapter presents Onegin through a double-

illumination of the author-narrator, as this author-narrator saw
him in 1819/20, and as Onegin appeared to him now, in 1823.

Chapter I of *Onegin* is made up chiefly of presenting a
typical day of Onegin's, and then a brief passage of the friendship of Onegin and the author-narrator just before both left St.
Petersburg. Onegin's day presents him participating in the
social whirl, but as one whose youthful impressionability and
ability to perceive and feel have been prematurely chilled, as
one who has become prematurely disenchanted and so remains.
Onegin's inability to feel is highlighted by the contrasting freshness and vitality of impression of the author-narrator. For example, the author-narrator shows the enjoyment that the finest
ballerina of the time, Istomina, could arouse in him (I use
Walter Arndt's translation, here and below):

> There stands ashimmer, half-ethereal,
> Submissive to the magisterial
> Magician's wand, amid her corps
> Of nymphs, Istómina—the floor
> Touched with one foot, the other shaping
> A slow-drawn circle, then—surprise—
> A sudden leap, and away she flies
> Like down from Aeol's lips escaping,
> Bends and unbends to rapid beat
> And twirling trills her tiny feet.   I.20

This may very well be the supreme example of motion-painting
in all Russian literature. In contrast to the author-narrator's vital
experience, Onegin comes in late, tramps over everybody's feet,
and after looking over the women and then the men, finally
glances absent-mindedly at the stage and yawns at the dancer
and the ballet.

A little farther on, the author-narrator starts Onegin off to a
ball, but does not bother even to present him there—because his
reactions, or his nonreactions, are predictable. Instead, in sharp
implied contrast to Onegin's "chilledness" of feeling, he presents perhaps the most famous "digression" of the entire work—

his own reminiscences on women's feet—which has the central passage:

> I watched the storm-foreboding ocean,
> With envy saw the waves repeat
> Their onrush of tumultuous motion
> To stretch in love about her feet;
> Then of their touch how I was aching
> With my own lips to be partaking!   I.33

Thus the disenchanted Onegin's perceptions, or rather nonperceptions, are contrasted with the vital memories of the author-narrator.

The passage on the author-narrator's friendship with Onegin, toward the end Chapter I, shows the attraction Onegin had held for him in 1820:

> He who has lived and thought can never
> Look on mankind without disdain;
> He who has felt is haunted ever
> By days that will not come again;
> No more for him enchantment's semblance,
> On him the serpent of remembrance
> Feeds, and remorse corrodes his heart.
> All this is likely to impart
> An added charm to conversation.
> At first, indeed, Onegin's tongue
> Used to abash me; but ere long
> I liked his acid derogation,
> His humor, half shot-through with gall,
> Grim epigrams' malicious drawl.   I.46

The passage shows the appeal Onegin had had for him, but the distancing comment in the middle ("all this is likely to impart an added charm to conversation") shows that, however appealing Onegin's disenchanted attitude may have been for him then, by the time of writing the chapter he has outgrown it. This also suggests that the fictional Onegin, at least in part, played the role of a "demon" to this author-narrator in 1820, but by 1823 this "demon"-induced disenchantment is over.

This means that the author-narrator's memories presented in the digressions in Chapter I are vital experiences of youthful enchantment relived through memory by one who has had an intermediate stage of disenchantment; hence, that their narrator is an author-narrator who has experienced mature "reenchantment." In turn, this means that the beautiful poetic digression on freedom (seen in terms of an escape to Italy) represents a "sublime theme" from "The Demon" seen from the point of view of mature reenchantment. At the same time, the positive qualities seen as present in Onegin in the passage on his friendship with this author-narrator show that there were things worth learning from Onegin.

Thus in Chapter I of *Onegin* the author-narrator's vital response to experience is in sharp contrast to Onegin's disenchantment and inability to respond. The author-narrator is in the third stage of maturing, a stage that provides the stance which continues throughout the novel. This is not all. I should like to suggest a point which I lack the space to develop here: that the key to understanding the multilevel continuing play of irony in *Onegin* has to do with how the author-narrator in the third stage, mature reenchantment, reacts to earlier stages of youthful enchantment and subsequent disenchantment and finds meaning not only in the first stage but also in the second.

4

Our final topic is a brief consideration of the relationship between the developmental stages of the author-narrator and the basic characterization of the two chief male characters of the novel, Onegin and Lensky. Though their characterization is in no sense merely schematic or allegorical, they nevertheless represent two individuals at different stages of the maturing process as seen above, with the implied question whether each of them has the potential of reaching maturity. They are imperfect, humanized, particularized representations of the "ideal" figures of the "young poet" and the "demon" in Pushkin's lyric "The Demon." Lensky is the enthusiastic, enchanted young man of eighteen to nineteen, the exalted poet of love and friendship. In terms of the novel his love for Olga is considered by our author-narrator as being appropriate for his age. Indeed, at Lensky's age, Pushkin himself had been writing a long poem, *Ruslan and Lyudmila,* in which the heroine (later spoken of directly in the novel as having been an incarnation of Pushkin's Muse) is like Olga in her charming feminine flightiness combined with feminine sensuality ready to be awakened. But he presents Olga as acting negatively on Lensky as his living Muse and suggests that for the poet to marry her (as permanent Muse) would foreclose his possible maturing as a poet. Onegin's deliberate arousing of Lensky's jealousy results for Lensky in disenchantment with friendship, as regards Onegin, and, temporarily, with love, as regards Olga. Lensky's temporary disenchantment with Olga is dispelled; his final poem, the night before his fatal duel, presents with terrible irony, in the context of the entire novel, the illusion of his trust that she will be faithful to him or his memory. Thus, for Lensky Onegin plays the role of "demon" and then of his actual slayer.

The novel had already suggested that Lensky is hardly the "ideal" poet of the lyric "The Demon." Pushkin always thought that a poet should be first a man, and then a poet. At first, Lensky is too much the poet—one who lives the role of poet all the time—the poet of only the ideal, of abstractions rather than perceptions. Then he becomes all too human, to the point of dubious taste, as is shown by his saying to Onegin of his affianced Olga: ". . . how splendid/Have Olga's shoulders grown, her bust!/ Ah, and her soul!" (IV.48). The author-narrator gives two possibilities for Lensky if he had survived the duel: He might have become a great poet with a "holy insight" to reveal; or, perhaps, after marriage he might have become an ex-poet, a cuckold, an idle landowner who would die of the gout at forty. The total novel suggests that Lensky, to become a great poet, would have had to survive Onegin's "demonic" temptation—which would have required more depth of character than he possessed. Thus he dies as poet because he lacks the potentiality for poetic maturity.

Onegin's characterization in the novel, from this point of view, is more complex. For Lensky (as perhaps for the younger author-narrator as fictional character in the novel), Onegin is, however inadvertently, a "demon," a tempter. For himself, Onegin represents a man who is arrested at the stage of disenchantment. There are definite suggestions that his disenchantment came too soon and has lasted too long. The novel points out a number of times that Onegin was no poet. At the same time, there are continuing hints that his cold disenchantment may not be permanent: in the brief passage of the liveliness of memories he shares with the author-narrator in Chapter I; in his reactions to Tatyana, even though he rejects her love; in his consciousness before the duel with Lensky, even though he participates in the duel and kills his antagonist in it. Thus by the final chapter of the novel we are prepared for the inevitable surprise of Onegin's recovering the ability to feel. In concentrated form, one stanza tells us what he feels, after he has fallen in love with the now married and inaccessible Tatyana:

> Imagination deals and shuffles
> Its rapid motley solitaires:
> He sees on melting snow-sheet dozing
> A lad, quite still, as if reposing
> Asleep upon a hostel bed,
> And someone says: "That's that—he's dead . . ."
> . . . .
> A rustic house—and who would be
> Framed in the window? . . . Who but She!   VIII.37

Again, the themes or their inversions are love and friendship, with Imagination centering on dead Lensky (betrayed friendship) and Tatyana by the window of her rural home (rejected love). The genuineness of Onegin's love for Tatyana is manifest from the fact that the Tatyana he sees in Imagination is not the grande dame in St. Petersburg, but the country miss. During the novel there is a continuing implied question whether Onegin will overcome his disenchantment. He indeed recovers the ability to feel love, so that he reaches at least a partial stage three; any further capacities for feeling Onegin may have gained or regained at the end of the novel are not revealed. We are not told what he may do with his new stage of maturity, when Tatyana has rejected his love just as he had earlier rejected hers.

Along with the theme of maturing in *Onegin* runs a central theme of a time for doing and a time for being. The stages of the author-narrator's development are suggested as the "natural" ones of the novel—youthful enchantment to twenty or so, then a period of disenchantment to twenty-three or twenty-four, but a mature reenchantment by that time. Lensky died at nineteen, at the first breath of disenchantment (and still in his illusion that Olga was his fated, faithful love). The precise time Onegin became disenchanted is not made clear; we learn only that it was "early." In the novel, he is some three years older than the author-narrator. Onegin first saw Tatyana in 1820, when he was twenty-four or so; he fell in love with her too late, in 1824/25, when he was twenty-eight or -nine. Pushkin was first "visited" by Tatyana as his Muse in 1823, when he was twenty-four, about the same age Onegin was when he met her. In terms of the developmental scale the novel presents, the unhappiness of both Tatyana and Onegin may be interpreted as resulting, at least in large part, from his being, when he first saw her, at a stage he should have already outgrown. Onegin did not "deserve" Tatyana, Pushkin is reported as having told a contemporary. This is true within the novel, first, because Onegin is no poet and hence did not deserve the "ideal" or Muse of a poet, and second—and this is more basic but related—because he prematurely succumbed to disenchantment and then was enthralled by it too long and too completely.

Critics often comment about Pushkin's moving toward *prose*

in *Onegin,* and, indeed, he comments to this effect within the novel. It is true that *Onegin* is not in a single, intense, "elevated" style (unlike his *Prisoner of the Caucasus*) and that some of its styles, while remaining poetic, suggest a poet's prose. But the prose of this style suggests Pushkin's familiar letters, not his "artistic prose." And it is true that in his thirties, Pushkin indeed wrote prose fiction—some of the finest in Russian—as well as poetry in various genres. But by no means are all the varied styles in *Onegin* prosaic in any sense. Pushkin never wrote poetry more lyrical than that of numerous of the passages in *Onegin.* An overemphasis on *prose* in interpreting the novel can, I think, lead toward a misunderstanding of the novel's attitude toward poetry and prose. Actually, the entire novel suggests the importance of being poetic. A basic—perhaps *the* basic—underlying question of the novel is not simply the stages of development, but how a poet (or the poetic in man) can develop to maturity and remain, or once more become, poetic. From this point of view, both chief male characters of the fictional story fail to "measure up," in that each insufficiently manifests the genuinely poetic. It is thus appropriate that the first great Russian novel should be in poetry and have its author-narrator adopt a poetic stance that can accept much that is usually considered prosaic and turn it into poetry: poetry of mature reenchantment. The later great nineteenth-century Russian novels were in prose, both in style and in the author's consciousness.

The Hierarchy of Narratees in Eugene Onegin[1]

SONA STEPHAN HOISINGTON

Works of literature are always directed toward an audience, yet paradoxically—to quote the title of Walter Ong's recent essay—"the writer's audience is always a fiction."[2] Just as we distinguish between the author of a literary work and the image the author creates of himself within a work, so must we distinguish between the real individual who reads a work and the fictitious person we become in the process of reading it. For, as Walker Gibson points out, "every time we open the pages of another piece of writing, we are embarked on a new adventure in which we become a new person—a person as controlled and definable and as remote from the chaotic self of daily life as the lover in a sonnet. Subject to the degree of our literary sensibility, we are recreated by the language. We assume, for the sake of the experience, that set of attitudes and qualities which the language asks us to assume, and if we cannot assume them, we throw the book away."[3] A text then places certain demands on us; it "imposes" a role on us. Successful reading depends upon our assuming that role, on our taking on the character of what I should like to call the "implied reader" created by the author.[4] This paper is addressed to the question of how we as readers role-play, or, more exactly, how a text guides and manipulates us so that we become the "implied reader." The case in point is Alexander Pushkin's narrative poem *Eugene Onegin*.

As Gerald Prince points out in his study of the narratee, the "reader" (*chitatel'*) is explicitly mentioned in *Eugene Onegin*, and the references are both frequent and direct.[5] The narrator

turns to the reader at the beginning of the work ("Onegin,
dobryi moy priyatel', / Rodilsya na bregakh Nevy, / Gde mozhet
byt' rodilis' vy, / Ili blistali, moy chitatel'," I.2) and bids him farewell at the conclusion (VIII.49). At first glance it would seem
that we are asked to become this "reader." Certainly in the
sentimental fiction of Pushkin's predecessor Nikolay Karamzin
the "reader" so addressed within the text coincides with the
"implied reader." [6] But is this true of Pushkin's work as well?
In order to answer this question let us examine the text of
Eugene Onegin, and let us begin with the final and most famous
address to the reader: [7]

> My reader—friend or not, whichever
> You were—now that the story's end
> Is here our mingled paths to sever,
> I want to leave you as a friend.
> Farewell. Whate'er you sought to capture
> In my loose rhymes—be it the rapture
> Of reminiscence, pause from toil,
> Lively tableaus, the piercing foil
> Of wit, or bits of faulty grammar—
> Please God you found here but a grain
> To conjure dreams, to entertain,
> To move the heart, to raise a clamor
> Of controversy in the press.
> Upon this note we part—God bless!   VIII.49

Ostensibly, this is a friendly farewell. The narrator—and here
I should like to suggest that in *Eugene Onegin* the narrator is
synonymous with the "implied author" [8]—appears deferential and
anxious to part with the reader on good terms. But then one
might ask why does he address the reader here as *ty?* Why
does he not use the more formal and also more respectful *vy?*
This is particularly puzzling in light of the fact that on every other
occasion the reader is addressed as *vy* (for example, in Chapter
I.2). Something else is puzzling here as well. The narrator says
with great deference that he hopes the reader is pleased with

the work, that it in some "small way" meets his expectations. But then in the catalogue that follows these expectations are in effect reduced to absurdity, as the text shifts abruptly and without warning from *ostrye slova* to *grammaticheskiye oshibki,* from *mechty* to *zhurnal'nye sshibki.* Both this reduction—a device used twice within a span of twelve lines—and the forced familiarity the narrator assumes, insisting all the while that the reader and he part as friends (significantly, *priyatel'* is used here rather than the more intimate form, *drug,* which we would expect), indicate the ironic nature of this stanza.[9] As implied reader we are required to reject the literal meaning and to "reconstruct" that meaning.[10] The "between-the-lines dialogue"[11] which emerges between implied author and implied reader might be paraphrased as follows: "You and I know this reader is no friend of mine or of my work. We recognize that he is a pompous ass and a literary philistine. Imagine, approaching my work looking for grammatical errors! You, on the other hand, share my values and beliefs. You are a discerning person and a literary connoisseur. You are a true friend of my work and, therefore, my true friend."

From the above analysis it is apparent that the implied reader should not be confounded with the "reader" so addressed within the work, or what I should like to call the "mock reader."[12] In fact, there is a great gulf between them. The mock reader addressed so deferentially by the narrator (now he is *chitatel' blagorodnyi,* IV.20; now *dostopochtennyi moy chitatel',* IV.22; now *chitatel' blagosklonnyi,* VII.5) is associated paradoxically with a whole set of values the implied author rejects. The implied reader is the narrator's real intimate, and a bond of intimacy is created by means of irony.[13] We find ourselves actively engaged in a "mutual performance" with the implied author.[14] The author offers us an "unequivocal invitation to reconstruct," and we are required to make a series of precise judgments.[15] This engagement draws the reader close to the author. As Wayne Booth puts it, "the author I infer behind the false words is my kind of man, because he enjoys playing with irony, because he

assumes *my* capacity for dealing with it and—most important—
because he grants me a kind of wisdom; he assumes that he
does not have to spell out the shared and secret truths on which
my reconstruction is built." [16] We have a "strong sense of reject-
ing a whole structure of meanings, a kind of world that the
author himself obviously rejects" and of moving to a higher
level where we share a kind of "knowledge" with the author.
"The movement is always toward an obscured point that is intended as wiser, wittier, more compassionate, subtler, truer, more
moral . . ."—to quote Booth once again.[17] Because we play an
active role in constructing this higher meaning, we find ourselves
committed to it. Standing firmly and securely with the implied
author, we look down upon the unknowing victims. In the
stanza we have just examined, the bond that is forged is that
much stronger because the mock reader is the object of the
irony and the "knowledge" we attain so flattering to our sense
of self-esteem.

But if the mock reader is a victim, what can be said about the
"friends" (*druz'ya*), that close circle of intimates to whom the
narrator tells his story? Although the mock reader clearly remains an outsider, distanced from the author by means of irony,
surely these friends must be insiders. After all, they have been
close to the poet-narrator for a long time (see, for example, IV.45:
". . . za nego [shampanskoye] / Poslednyi bednyi lept, byvalo,/
Daval ya. Pomnite l', druz'ya? / Ego volshebnaya struya/ Rozh-
dala glupostey ne malo,/ A skol'ko shutok i stikhov,/ I sporov i
veselykh snov!"). They are interested in his poetry and the loves
that inspire it. Significantly, they chat with the narrator, while
the mock reader maintains a hostile silence:

> These days I often listen to
> A certain question, friends, from you:
> "For whom, then, languishes your lyre?
> Among the maiden's jealous throng,

To whom do you inscribe your song?"

"Whose gazes, kindling inspiration,
Have recompensed from melting eyes
Your meditative incantation?
Whom did your verse immortalize?"   I.57–58

The poet treats them as confidants, to them he reveals his thoughts and feelings (see, for example, "Akh, brattsy! Kak ya byl dovolen,/ Kogda tserkvey i kolokolen,/ Sadov, chertogov polukrug/ Otkrylsya predo mnoyu vdrug!,"VII.36). He addresses them endearingly as *brattsy* (VII.36), *bratya* (IV.37), and repeatedly calls them affectionately *milyi* (I.32;III.30;III.41;VI.46).

Who are these "friends," the intimate circle with whom the poet-narrator chats cozily and in whom he so readily confides? Pushkin first identifies the group by focusing attention on an absent member:

O bard of feasts and languid sorrow,
Would that you were still with me here,
I should have boldly sought to borrow
Your magic for a spell, my dear:
To see in your bewitching cadence
New-rendered my impassioned maiden's
Bizarre epistolary flight!
Where are you? Come: my prior right;
I make it over to you gladly . . .
But, weaned his heart from human praise,
Amid portentous cliffs he strays
'Neath Finland's heaven low'ring sadly,
A lonesome wand'rer, and his soul
Does not perceive my grievous dole.   III.30

Lest there be any doubt as to identity of this *pevets*, Pushkin identifies him in a note as Eugene Baratynsky. (Apropos of this, it should be pointed out that the mock reader, on the other hand, is never identified other than as *chitatel'*. In fact, in

Chapter VIII.49, analyzed above, the narrator claims he has no idea who this *chitatel'* is.) On the basis of Chapter III.30, we infer that the "friends" are Pushkin's fellow poets, the well-known Pushkin Pleiad. That same audience is found in Pushkin's epistles (for example, "Baratynskomu," 1822, "K Yazykovu," 1824, "Iz Pis'ma k Vyazemskomu," 1825). Baratynsky is fictionalized here in a manner reminiscent of that genre. He is portrayed as a poet, and allusions are made to his poetic works. The forms of address (*pevets, milyi moy*), the bantering tone, the "request" are also characteristic of the epistle. In that genre these devices work to bring speaker and audience together, to convey the notion that they are men of the same stripe.[18] To quote Pushkin's epistle to Vyazemsky: "No milyi—muzy nashi sestry,/ Itak, ty vse zhe bratets moy." (As has been pointed out, in *Eugene Onegin* the "friends" are addressed as *brattsy* and *bratya*.) In Pushkin's epistles the underlying assumption is that a certain kinship exists between speaker and audience because they are both poets. But is the same assumption operative in *Eugene Onegin?* In Chapter III.30, does the poet-narrator identify with Baratynsky as a fellow poet, or does he set himself apart from *Pevets Pirov* and, by implication, from "the group" as a whole?

This question is answered in Chapter V.3, where the relationship between poet-narrator, mock reader, friends, and implied reader is clarified. In the opening lines the implied author stops the mock reader short, grabs him by the lapels, and accuses him openly of not liking his poetry: "No mozhet byt', takogo roda/ Kartiny vas ne privlekut:/ Vse èto nizkaya priroda;/Izyashchnogo ne mnogo tut." In the next breath the author insists that the mock reader likes the "refined" poetry of "the group": "Sogrety vdokhnoven'ya bogom,/ Drugoy poèt roskoshnym slogom/Zhivopisal nam pervy sneg/I vse ottenki zimnikh neg:/ On vas plenit, ya v tom uveren,/ Risuya v plamennykh stikhakh/Progulki taynye v sanyakh." In the notes Pushkin identifies not only the poet (Vyazemsky) but the work as well ("First Snow"). Thus, the Pleiad poets and their poetry are linked with the mock reader. We are told that he will be "captivated" by their verses. But where exactly does the narrator stand vis-à-vis the "friends"? The answer emerges in the final lines of the stanza: "No ya borot'sya ne nameren/ Ni s nim pokamest', ni s toboy,/ Pevets Finlyandki molodoy!" (Again, not only is the poet identified—Baratynsky—but the work as well—*Eda*.) This disavowal is clearly ironic in light of the fact that the narrator has already drawn a line between "himself" and "the group." It indicates that he really regards his friends as poetic rivals. In this stanza he is conducting a polemic against the kind of poetry his friends write, and we as implied reader are cleverly manipulated into taking his side. How is this accomplished? We are "put on the spot," our loyalties "tested." "Perhaps," the narrator insists coyly, "you don't like my poetry. Most assuredly you prefer the verses of Vyazemsky and Baratynsky." Note the strategic use here of *mozhet byt'* and *ya v tom uveren*. Pushkin tricks us. Before we realize what has happened, we find ourselves protesting warmly that we do indeed like the narrator's poetry and genuinely believing that his poetry is, in fact, superior to that of "the group." Again it is by means of irony that we are engaged and manipulated. The device, however, works in a different manner than in Chapter VIII.49. For here we hasten to join the implied author, afraid that otherwise we too will become the object of ridicule. Once reassured that we have not lost our "privileged position," [19] we can look down on mock reader and poet-friends alike, aware that these friends too are "fictive" and secure in the "knowledge" that we as implied reader are the true friend.

Does this complete the hierarchy of narratees in *Eugene Onegin,* or is the matter more complex? Are mock reader and mock friends equidistant from implied author, or is there a pecking order here as well? In an attempt to answer this question let us examine three passages from Chapter VI. The poet Lensky has impetuously challenged Onegin to a duel, angered by his friend's flirtations with Olga, his bride-to-be. Onegin is afraid of being ridiculed if he does not fight. He accepts Lensky's challenge and then deliberately shoots and kills his young friend. Following the description of the duel, Pushkin explores the implications of Lensky's death and, in so doing, gives the response of each narratee to this event. First let us look at the reaction of the mock reader or, more precisely, the reaction attributed to him: "no chto by ni bylo, chitatel',/ Uvy, lyubovnik molodoy,/ Poèt, zadumchivyi mechtatel',/ Ubit priyatel'skoy rukoy!" (VI.40). It is easy to see the mock reader wringing his hands and exclaiming, "How awful!" The intensity of his outburst is underscored both by the interjection *uvy* and by the final exclamation point. The mock reader certainly assumes the proper pose, but is there anything more to it than this? We quickly deduce that, because he makes so much of it, his concern is completely artificial and that it simply masks a feeling of total indifference. In actual fact, the mock reader, while making a big to-do about Lensky's death, is not moved by the event at all. His real sympathies lie with Onegin, who is as self-centered and as much a conformist as he himself.[20]

How do the mock friends respond to Lensky's death? Are they also so insensitive to what has happened? No, to the contrary, they are grieved that Lensky has died. Here is their, as it were, "collective" lament:

> My friends, you will lament the poet
> Who, flowering with a happy gift,
> Must wilt before he could bestow it
> Upon the world, yet scarce adrift
> From boyhood's shore. Now he will never
> Seethe with that generous endeavor,
> Those storms of mind and heart again,
> Audacious, tender, or humane!
> Stilled now are love's unruly urges,
> The thirst for knowledge and for deeds,
> Contempt for vice and what it breeds,
> And stilled you too, ethereal surges,
> Breath of a transcendental clime,
> Dreams from the sacred realm of rhyme! VI.36

It is evident from the stanza that the friends view Lensky as a fellow poet and that they mourn his passing as such. The emphasis is on the untimeliness of the loss; the implication is that Lensky was destined to "flower" into a great poet. In contrast to the mock reader, the poet-friends are genuinely moved by Lensky's death. Without question their sympathy is sincere, but is it not misplaced? Is Lensky's death truly a great loss to poetry? In Chapter VI.39, which follows the friends' lament, Pushkin projects a very ordinary fate for Lensky, telling us that he perhaps would have "parted with the muses" and settled down to a run-of-the-mill life in the country. This prosaic future seems, in fact, more in keeping with Lensky's character than the lofty fate imagined by the poet-friends. For Lensky is not a gifted poet but a naïve young man who writes derivative verse. His future plans included marriage to a very ordinary young lady, Olga, who undoubtedly would have become the petty tyrant her mother is. Given the "precarious" nature of youthful enthusiasm and the deadening effect of routine, it seems very likely that Lensky would in the end have idled away his life in a quilted dressing gown. Appropriately, the lot Pushkin projects for Lensky is reminiscent of the life of Olga's father, Dmitri Larin. Even the details are the same: the dressing gown, the idle life, the excessive attention to eating and drinking, the complacency, and the uneventful death (see Chapter II.34–36).

It is impossible to separate the lament of the poet-friends from the idiom in which it is written. The style is that of the elegy, that genre associated with both Lensky and the poet-friends. (In Chapter IV.31, Pushkin actually compares Lensky's elegies to those of "group" member Yazkyov.) In the lament we find such conventional elegiac images as "bloom" (*tsvet*) and "withered" (*uvyal*). In the context of the work these metaphors seem inappropriate, terribly contrived, and, in the final analysis, patently false. After all Lensky did not "wither" away in the "bloom" of youth. He was a rash young man who was killed in cold blood by a friend. In the lament, significantly, there is no allusion to how Lensky died, no hint that he was murdered.

In Chapter VI.36, once again we are faced with irony, but the irony here is more complex. For we find not only "internal" irony but dramatic irony as well. The lament is overdone, something Pushkin calls attention to by parallelism (*gde, gde, gde* and *vy, vy, vy*) and by enjambment (the latter device is used to ridicule the elegiac image *uvyal*). The lament, however, is not only out of tune in and of itself, it is also off-key in the larger context of the work. For, as already observed, there is an ironic contrast between the conventional motifs employed in the lament and the reality of Lensky's death. Through this set of ironies Pushkin successfully discredits the style of "the group" in the eyes of the implied reader.

How finally does the implied author demand that we the implied reader respond to Lensky's death? Clearly not with a shrug of the shoulders or with effusive outpourings. On the contrary, we are required to play a quite different role. We are put in the position of the friend who kills and made to experience the duel from his perspective:

> What if your pistol-shot has shattered
> The temple of a dear young boy,
> Who, flushed with drinking, may have scattered
> Rash words at random to annoy,
> Sly looks or inadvertent slander;
> Or has himself in sudden dander
> Incontinently called you out:
> I dare say there is little doubt
> Your feelings on the point would differ
> On that chill dawn when he is found,
> Death on his brow, upon the ground,
> When, cold already, growing stiffer,
> Before your starting eyes he sprawls,
> Quite deaf to your despairing calls!   VI.34

Pushkin focuses our attention on the act itself, and he demands that we view this act as something awful, horrible because of its finality. He makes us realize that Lensky's death is terrible not because it is a tremendous loss to poetry but because it is out-and-out murder. He compels us the implied reader to make a moral judgment.[21]

To conclude, in *Eugene Onegin* proper responses are elicited from the implied reader largely through the use of irony. The implied reader must learn to recognize the ironic intent of the implied author and "reconstruct" literal meanings by making precise judgments. As an integral part of this "training" he is invited to assume various mock roles which he must necessarily reject. The victims of the irony, those who are deceived by it and become its object, are the two mock audiences: poet-friends and reader. Each of these mock audiences is identified with one of the work's central characters: poet-friends with fellow poet Lensky and reader with that contemporary fellow Petersburgite, Onegin. The hierarchy of narratees that emerges then is a complex one, the scheme threefold in nature. Implied author and implied reader stand firmly and securely together and from above look down on the misguided "friends," poetic "brothers" to Lensky. Below them yet, unaware that he is at the very bottom of the heap, struts the complacent "reader," that close comrade of Onegin.

NOTES

1. This essay was first published in *Canadian-American Slavic Studies,* 10, No. 2 (Summer 1976), pp. 242–249. An earlier version was presented at a session of the AAASS meeting in 1975. The author wishes to thank Professor Robert Belknap, who chaired that session, for first drawing her attention to the problem of the "reader" in fiction.

2. W. J. Ong, "The Writer's Audience Is Always a Fiction," *PMLA,* 90 (1975), pp. 9–21.

3. W. Gibson, "Authors, Speakers, Readers, and Mock Readers," *College English,* 11 (1949–50), p. 265.

4. The term is Wayne Booth's. See his *Rhetoric of Irony* (Chicago and London: University of Chicago Press, 1974), p. 233.

5. G. Prince, "Introduction à l'étude du narrataire," *Poétique*, 14 (1973), p. 187.

6. In Karamzin's stories the "reader," like the narrator, is cast in the role of a "sensitive soul" ("Natal'ya, Boyarskaya Doch'"), one who "knows his own heart" ("Bednaya Liza").

7. Prince alludes to this stanza in his article "On Readers and Listeners in Narrative," *Neophilologus*, 55 (1971), p. 119.

8. Again, the term is Wayne Booth's. See his *Rhetoric of Fiction* (Chicago and London: University of Chicago Press, 1961), p. 75.

9. Prince does not take this irony into consideration. Is he then successful in assuming the role of implied reader?

10. The metaphor is Booth's. See *Rhetoric of Irony*, p. 33.

11. Gibson, *loc. cit.*, p. 266.

12. The term is my own. Although critics have discussed this problem (i.e. Prince, *loc. cit.*, pp. 191–92), to my knowledge no critic has suggested a term which would call attention to this distinction. When Walker Gibson used "mock reader," he had in mind the implied reader (see "Authors, Speakers, Readers, and Mock Readers," *loc. cit.*). Significantly, he later repudiated the term, arguing that it was "misleading" (*Tough, Sweet, and Stuffy* [Bloomington, Ind.: Indiana University Press, 1966], p. 166). It seems to me, however, that here it is appropriate.

13. I am deeply indebted to Booth's *Rhetoric of Irony* for many of the ideas and terms used in the following discussion.

14. *Ibid.*, p. 39.

15. *Ibid.*, p. 233.

16. *Ibid.*, p. 28.

17. *Ibid.*, p. 36.

18. N. G., "Poslaniye," *Literaturnaya èntsiklopediya*, 10 vols. (Moscow: Kommunisticheskaya Akademiya, 1929–39), IX, pp. 171–72; M. L. Gasparov, "Poslaniye," *Kratkaya literaturnaya èntsiklopediya*, 8 vols. (Moscow: Sovetskaya èntsiklopediya, 1962–75), V, p. 905.

19. W. Iser, "Indeterminacy and the Reader's Response in Prose Fiction," in J. H. Miller, ed., *Aspects of Narrative* (New York: Columbia University Press, 1971), p. 29.

20. Significantly, when Onegin spurns Tatyana's attentions, the mock reader approves of his behavior (IV.18), while the implied reader is made to realize that Onegin does not reveal "nobility of soul," that, in fact, his behavior is motivated by a sterile egotism.

21. Significantly, the response of the implied reader is elicited first (for the sake of the argument I reversed the order of the three

responses). Unlike Dostoevsky, Pushkin does not "let" us experience doubts. He carefully secures moral judgment from us as implied reader and only then introduces us to the reactions of the other narratees. Thereby, he ensures that we will grasp the inappropriateness of the one response, the hypocrisy of the other, and the irony of both.

Unmindful of the proud world's pleasure,
But friendship's claim alone in view,
I wish I could have brought a treasure
Far worthier to pledge to you:
Fit for a soul of beauty tender,
By sacred visitations taught
To blend in rhyme of vivid splendor
Simplicity and lofty thought;
Instead—to your kind hands I render
The motley chapters gathered here,
At times amusing, often doleful,
Blending the rustic and the soulful,
Chance harvest of my pastimes dear,
Of sleepless moods, light inspirations,
Fruit of my green, my withered years,
The mind's dispassionate notations,
The heart's asides, inscribed in tears.[1]

*Chapter
One*

He is in haste to live and hies himself to feel.

K. VYAZEMSKY

I. 1

"Now that he is in grave condition,
My uncle, decorous old dunce,[2]
Has won respectful recognition;
And done the perfect thing for once.
His action be a guide to others;
But what a bore, I ask you, brothers,
To tend a patient night and day
And venture not a step away:
Is there hypocrisy more glaring
Than to amuse one all but dead,
Shake up the pillow for his head,
Dose him with melancholy bearing,
And think behind a public sigh:
'Deuce take you, step on it and die!' "

I. 2

Thus a young good-for-nothing muses,
As in the dust the post-wheels spin,
By a decree of sovereign Zeus's
The extant heir to all his kin.
Friends of Ruslan and of Lyudmila![3]
Allow me, with no cautious feeler
Or foreword, to present at once
The hero of my new romance:
Onegin, a dear friend of mine,
Born where Nevá flows, and where you,
I daresay, gentle reader, too
Were born, or once were wont to shine;
There I myself once used to be:
The North, though, disagrees with me.[4]

I. 3

Fresh from a blameless state career,
His father lived on IOU's,
He used to give three balls a year,
Until he had no more to lose.
Fate treated young Onegin gently:
Madame first watched him competently,
From her *Monsieur* received the child;
The boy was likable, though wild.
Monsieur, a poor *abbé* from Paris,
To spare the youngster undue strain,
Would teach him in a playful vein,
With moral strictures rarely harass,
Reprove him mildly for each lark,
And walk him in the Summer Park.

I. 4

But when young manhood's stormy morrow
Broke in due course for young Eugene,
The age of hope and tender sorrow,
Monsieur was driven from the scene.
This left Eugene in free possession;
Clad in a London dandy's fashion,
With hair style of the latest cast,
He joined Society at last.
In writing and in conversation
His French was perfect, all allowed;
He danced Mazurkas well and bowed
Without constraint or affectation.
Enough! Society's verdict ran:
A bright and very nice young man.

I. 5

Since we pick up our education
In bits and pieces here and there,
To earn a brilliant reputation
With us, thank God, is no affair.
It was conceded he had learning
(By judges ruthless and discerning),
Though of a somewhat bookish drift;
For he possessed the happy gift
Of unaffected conversation:
To skim one topic here, one there,
Keep silent with an expert's air
In too exacting disputation,
And with a flash of sudden quips
Charm tender smiles to tender lips.

I. 6

The Latin vogue has now receded,
And I must own that, not to brag,
He had what knowledge may be needed
To puzzle out a Latin tag,
Flaunt Juvenal in a discussion,
Add "Vale" to a note in Russian;
Of the *Aeneid*, too, he knew,
With some mistakes, a line or two.
To burrow in the dusty pages
Of Clio's chronologic waste
Was hardly to our hero's taste;
But anecdotes of bygone ages,
From Romulus to days just past,
To these his memory clung fast.

I. 7

To hold life cheap for Sound,[5] he never
Experienced the sacred curse:
Do what we would, he took forever
Iambic for trochaic verse.
Homer, Theocritus disdaining,
From Adam Smith he sought his training
And was no mean economist;
That is, he could present the gist
Of how states prosper and stay healthy
Without the benefit of gold,
The secret being that, all told,
The *basic staples* make them wealthy.
His father failed to understand,
And mortgaged the ancestral land.

I. 8

Eugene's attainments were far vaster
Than I can take the time to show,
But where he really was a master,
Where he knew all there is to know,
What early meant in equal measure
His toil, his torment, and his pleasure,
What occupied at every phase
The leisured languor of his days,
Was the pursuit of that Fair Passion
Which Ovid sang, and for its sake
Was doomed to drain, in mutinous ache,
His glittering life's remaining ration
'Mid deaf Moldavia's cloddish loam,
Far from his dear Italian home.

(I. 9)[6]

I. 10

How soon he learnt to feign emotion,
Act hopeless grief or jealous pet,
To smother or foment devotion,
Seem steeped in melancholy, fret,
By turns disdainful and obedient,
Cool or attentive, as expedient!
How glum he was with gloom intense,
How flushed with flaming eloquence,
How casual-kind a letter-sender!
One end in view, one seeking most,
How utterly he was engrossed!
How nimble was his glance and tender,
Bold-shy, and when the time was near,
Agleam with the obedient tear!

I. 11

Forever new and interesting,
He scared with ready-made despair,
Amazed the innocent with jesting,
With flattery amused the fair,
Seized the chance instant of compliance
To sway ingenuous youth's defiance
By ardor or astute finesse,
Lure the spontaneous caress,
Implore, nay, force a declaration,
Ambush the first-note of the heart,
Flush Love from cover, and then dart
To fix a secret assignation . . .
And after that, to educate
His prey in private tête-à-tête!

I. 12

How soon he could arouse to hunger
The seasoned flirt's quiescent heart!
What ruthless scandal would he monger
Once he resolved with poisoned dart
To bring about a rival's ruin!
What snares he laid for his undoing!
Yet you, blithe husbands, by Fate's whim
Remain on friendly terms with him:
Him of all men the shrewd spouse fawns on,
Post-graduate of Faublas' school,
And the most skeptical old fool
And the bombastic ass with horns on,
Contented ever with his life,
Himself, his dinner, and his wife.

(I. 13, 14)

I. 15

The social notes are brought in gently,
While he is rising, or before.
What—invitations? Evidently;
Three for a single night, what's more.
A ball here, there a children's party;
Which will he skip to, our young hearty?
Which take up first now, let us see . . .
No matter—he can do all three.
Meanwhile there's boulevard parading:
Eugene, in faultless morning trim
And *Bolivar*[7] with ample brim,
Drives out and joins the promenading,
Till the repeater's watchful peal
Recalls him to the midday meal.

I. 16

Nightfall; the sleigh receives him. Listen:
He's off to shouts of "way—away!"
His beaver collar starts to glisten
With hoarfrost dusting, silver-gray.
On to Talon's,[8] pace unabating,
Kaverin[9] will no doubt be waiting.
He enters: corks begin to fly,
The Comet's[10] vintage gushes high,
Here roast beef oozes bloody juices,
And near that flower of French cuisine,
The truffle, youth's delight, is seen
The deathless pie Strasbourg produces,
Mid Limburger's aroma bold
And the pineapple's luscious gold.

I. 17

Their thirst for yet more goblets clamors
To douse the sizzling cutlet grease,
But the repeater's jingling hammers
Bid them to the new ballet piece.
The stage's arbiter, exacting,
Who to the charming queens of acting
His fervent, fickle worship brings,
Established freeman of the wings,
Eugene, of course, must not be missing
Where everyone without *faux pas*
Is free to cheer an *entrechat*,
Jeer Cleopatra, Phèdre, with hissing,
Call out Moïna (in a word,
Make sure that he is seen and heard).

I. 18[11]

Ah, Fairyland! In former season
He who was satire's paladin,
He shone there, Freedom's friend, Fonvízin,
And the deft mimicker, Knyazhnín.
There Ozeróv in national audits
Reaped ample toll of tears and plaudits
With young Semyónova to share;
Corneille's majestic muse was there
By our Katénin newly rendered;
There did the mordant Shakhovskoy
His riotous comedies deploy,
There to Did'lot were laurels tendered,
There, in the backdrops' shady maze,
I whiled away my youthful days.

I. 19

My goddesses! Speak, have you vanished?
Oh, hearken to my plaintive call:
Are you the same? Have others banished
And barred, yet not replaced you all?
Will yet with choral part-song capture,
With aerial spirit-flight enrapture,
Our Russian-born Terpsichore?
Or will the listless eye not see
On tedious stage familiar faces,
Scan with distraught binoculars
An alien world bereft of stars;
Cool witness to those heady graces,
Shall I be yawning at the cast
And mutely hanker for the past?

I. 20

The house is full, the box-tier glitters,
The pit, the stalls—all seethes and stirs;
Impatient clapping from the sitters
On high: the rising curtain whirs.
There stands ashimmer, half-ethereal,
Submissive to the magisterial
Magician's wands, amid her corps
Of nymphs Istómina[12]—the floor
Touched with one foot, the other shaping
A slow-drawn circle, then—surprise—
A sudden leap, and away she flies
Like down from Aeol's lip escaping,
Bends and unbends to rapid beat
And twirling trills her tiny feet.

I. 21

arrived late

Applause all round. Onegin enters
And threads his way from toe to toe.
His double spyglass swoops and centers
On box-seat belles he does not know.
All tiers his scrutiny embraces,
He's seen it all: the gowns and faces
Seemed clearly to fatigue his sight;
He traded bows on left and right
With gentlemen, at length conceded
An absent gaze at the ballet,
Then with a yawn he turned away
And spoke: "In all things change is needed;
On me ballets have lost their hold;
Didelot himself now leaves me cold."

I. 22   *leaves early*

While yet the cupids, devils, monkeys
Behind the footlights prance and swoop;
While yet the worn-out grooms and flunkies
Sleep on their furs around the stoop;
While yet they have not finished clapping.
Nose-blowing, coughing, hissing, tapping;
While yet the lanterns everywhere
Inside and outside shed their glare;
While yet chilled horses yank the tether
And, harness-weary, champ the bit,
And coachmen round the bonfires sit,
And, cursing, beat their palms together:
Onegin has already gone
To put his evening costume on.

I. 23

Oh, will it be within my powers
To conjure up the private den
Where Fashion's acolyte spent hours
To dress, undress, and dress again?
What London makes for cultured whimsy
Of novelties polite and flimsy,
And ships upon the Baltic brine
To us for tallow and for pine,
All that Parisian modish passion
And earnest industry collect
To tempt the taste of the elect
With comfort and caress of fashion,
Adorned the boudoir of our green
Philosopher at age eighteen.

I. 24

Bronze-work and china on the table,
An ambered hookah from Stambul,
Spirits in crystal bottles able
To soothe the brow with scented cool;
Steel files and little combs unending,
And scissors straight and scissors bending,
And brushes—recollection fails—
For hair and teeth and fingernails.
Rousseau—please pardon this digression—
Could not conceive how solemn Grimm[13]
Dared clean his nails in front of *him*,
Great bard of silver-tongued obsession.
Our champion of Man's liberties
Here surely was too hard to please!

I. 25

One can be capable and moral
With manicure upon one's mind:
Why vainly chide one's age and quarrel?
Custom is lord of all mankind.
Chadáyev-like, [14] Eugene was zealous,
Forestalling censure by the jealous,
To shun the least sartorial flaws—
A *swell*, as the expression was.
He used to squander many an hour
Before the mirrors in his room,
At last to issue forth abloom
Like playful Venus from her bower,
When in a man's disguise arrayed,
The goddess joins a masquerade.

I. 26

Now that this modish apparition
Has drawn your casual interest,
With the discerning world's permission,
I might describe how he was dressed;
I'd do it not without compunction,
Though to describe is my true function,
But *pantalons, gilet,* and *frack*—
With such words Russian has no truck,
For as it is, I keep inviting
Your censure for the way I use
Outlandish words of many hues
To deck my humble style of writing;
Though once I used to draw upon
The Academic Lexicon.

I. 27

But never mind this—we must hurry,
For while I wander off the track,
Onegin in a headlong flurry
Drives to the ball by hired hack.
Along the housefronts past him speeding,
Down streets aslumber, fast receding,
The double carriage lanterns bright
Shed their exhilarating light
And brush the snow with rainbow flutters;
With sparkling lampions, row on row,
The splendid mansion stands aglow;
In shadow-play across the shutters
Flit profile heads of demoiselles
And fashionably well-groomed swells.

I. 28

Now he has passed the liveried sentry,
Skipped up by every other stair
And, pausing at the marbled entry
To realign a straying hair,
Has entered. The great hall is swarming,
The band benumbed by its own storming,
In hum and hubbub, tightly pent,
The crowd's on the Mazurka bent;
Spurs ring, sparks glint from guardsmen's shoulders,
Belles' shapely feet and ankles sleek
Whirl by, and in their passing wreak
Much flaming havoc on beholders,
And fiddle music skirls and drowns
Sharp gibes of wives in modish gowns.

I. 29

When ardent dreams and dissipations
Were with me still, I worshiped balls:
No safer place for declarations,
Or to deliver tender scrawls.
Beware, you estimable spouses,
Look to the honor of your houses!
I wish you well, and so here goes
An earnest word from one who knows . . .
And you, Mamás of daughters, leaven
Your wits and shelter well your pets,
Keep straight and polished your lorgnettes!
Or else . . . or else, oh, gracious Heaven!
Such sound advice comes to my tongue
Because I haven't sinned so long.

I. 30

I burnt so much of life's brief candle
In levity I now regret!
Still, balls—but for the moral scandal
They breed, I should adore them yet.
I thrill to ardent youth's outpouring,
The crush and blaze, the spirit's soaring,
Those beauties artfully arrayed;
I love their feet—though I'm afraid
Throughout our land you won't discover
Three pairs of shapely female feet.
Ah—one I long could not delete
From memory . . . and still they hover,
Burnt-out and sad as I may be,
About my dreams and trouble me.

I. 31

When, where, what wildernesses threading
Will you forget them, luckless clown?
Dear little feet, where are you treading
The wildflowers of a vernal down?
Soft skies of Orient nurtured under,
On snowsheets of our northern tundra
You never left the faintest trace.
No, the luxurious embrace
Of yielding carpets did you treasure.
Has it been long I ceased to rue
My home, my freedom over you,
Forgot my greed for fame and pleasure?
Youth's happy years have waned, alas—
Like your light footprints in the grass.

I. 32

The breast of Dian, I adore it,
And Flora's cheek to me is sweet!
And yet I would not barter for it
Terpsichore's enchanting feet.
For they, the captive gaze ensnaring
With pledge of bliss beyond comparing,
Inveigle with their token charm
Desires' unbridled, wanton swarm.
These, friend Elvina, I admire—
By tablecovers half concealed,
In springtime on an emerald field,
In winter, propped before a fire,
When over gleaming floors they flee
Or stand on boulders by the sea.

I. 33

I watched the storm-foreboding ocean,
With envy saw the waves repeat
Their onrush of tumultuous motion
To stretch in love about her feet;
Then of their touch how I was aching
With my own lips to be partaking!
Ah—never, even in the blaze
Of early youth's tumultuous days,
Was I so racked with the desire
A kiss on maiden lips to claim,
On cheeks on which the roses flame,
On breasts astir with sultry fire;
No, never passion's gusts have wrought
A like destruction in my thought!

I. 34

I recollect one more such passion—
At times, in daydreams full of balm,
I hold glad hands out, stirrup-fashion—
And feel a foot cupped in my palm;
And still from these bewitching touches
Imagination seethes, clutches
The withered heart with fire again
Once more in love, once more in pain! . . .
But silence now—the garrulous lyre
Has praised those haughty ones enough;
In vain the odes which they inspire,
In vain the transports, which they scoff!
Their speeches and their glances sweet
At last deceive you . . . like their feet.

I. 35

But what about Onegin? Nodding,
He's driven homeward from the ball,
While drumbeats have long since been prodding
To life the strenuous capital.
The peddler struts, the merchant dresses,
The cabman to the market presses,
With jars the nimble milkmaids go,
Their footsteps crunching in the snow.
The cheerful morning sounds and hustles
Begin, shops open, stacks have puffed
Tall trunks of slate-blue smoke aloft;
The baker, punctual German, bustles
White-capped behind his service hatch
And more than once has worked the latch.

I. 36

But, worn-out by the ballroom's clamor,
And making midnight out of dawn,
The child of luxury and glamour
Sleeps tight, in blissful shade withdrawn.
At noon or so he wakes—already
Booked up till next dawn, in a steady
Motley routine of ceaseless play:
Tomorrow will be like Today.
In youth's bloom, free of prohibition,
With brilliant conquests to his name,
Each day a feast, his life a game,
Was he content with his condition?
Or was he hearty and inane
Amid carousals—but in vain?

I. 37

Yes—feeling early cooled within him;
He came to loathe that worldly grind;
Proud beauties could no longer win him
And uncontested rule his mind;
Constant inconstancy turns dreary;
Of friends and friendship he grew weary:
One can't forever and again
Chase with a bottle of champagne
Beefsteak and Strasbourg liver pasty
And scatter insults all around
When senses swim and temples pound:
And so, although by temper hasty,
Our lad at length was overfed
With taunts and duels, sword and lead.

I. 38

A malady to whose causation
We have, alas, as yet no clues,
Known as the Spleen to Albion's nation,
In the vernacular: the Blues—
With this disease he was infected;
He never, thank the Lord, projected
To put a bullet through his brain;
But life-at-large now seemed inane;
Wry, gloomy, with Childe Harold vying,
He seemed to languish in *salons,*
No worldly gossip, no *Bostóns,*[15]
Nor tender glance, nor wanton sighing,
Henceforward seemed to touch a string;
He ceased to notice anything.

(I. 39, 40, 41)

I. 42[16]

O weird and wondrous lionesses!
It's you he first of all forswore;
And high-life manners, one confesses,
These days are really quite a bore.
Although at times some well-born charmers
Talk Say and Bentham at us farmers,
Their conversation on the whole
Is hard to bear, however droll.
And what is worse, they are so stainless,
So lofty, so intelligent,
So piously benevolent,
So preternaturally swainless,
So circumspect and epicene,
Their very sight brings on the Spleen.

I. 43

And you, too, beauteous young sirens,
Whose forward cabs begin to cruise,
As night advances, the environs
Of Petersburg's great avenues,
Desist! Eugene has had his measure.
Apostate from the whirl of pleasure,
He has withdrawn into his den
And, yawning, reached for ink and pen.
He tried to write—from such tenacious
Endeavor, though, his mind recoiled;
And so the paper stayed unsoiled,
And he stayed out of that vivacious
Fraternity I don't condemn
Because, you see, I'm one of them.

I. 44

Next, still to indolence a victim,
His vacant soul to languor prone,
A laudable temptation pricked him
To make what others thought his own.
In scores of books, arrayed on shelving,
He read and read—in vain all delving:
Here length, there raving or pretense,
This one lacked candor, that one sense;
All had, each in its way, miscarried;
That which was old, was obsolete,
And what was new, with old replete;
Like first his women, he now buried
His books, and veiled their huddled shape
On dusty shelf with mourning crape.

I. 45

Of worldly bustle and unreason
I'd shed the burden, as had he,
And we became good friends that season.
His features fascinated me,
His bent for dreamy meditation,
His strangeness, free of affectation,
His frigidly dissecting mind.
He was embittered, I maligned;
We both had drunk from Passion's chalice:
In either, life had numbed all zest;
Extinct the glow in either breast;
For both, too, lay in wait the malice
Of reckless fortune and of man,
When first our lease of life began.

I. 46

He who has lived and thought can never
Look on mankind without disdain;
He who has felt is haunted ever
By days that will not come again;
No more for him enchantment's semblance,
On him the serpent of remembrance
Feeds, and remorse corrodes his heart.
All this is likely to impart
An added charm to conversation.
At first, indeed, Onegin's tongue
Used to abash me; but ere long
I liked his acid derogation,
His humor, half shot-through with gall,
Grim epigrams' malicious drawl.

I. 47

How often summer's radiant shimmer
Glowed over the Nevá at night,
Her cheerful mirror not aglimmer
With Dian's image—and the sight
Would hold us there in rapt reflection,
Aware again in recollection
Of love gone by, romance of yore;
Carefree and sentient once more,
We savored then, intoxicated,
The night's sweet balm in mute delight!
As some fair dream from prison night
The sleeping convict may deliver
To verdant forests—fancy-lorn
We reveled there at life's young morn.

I. 48

His soul in rueful agitation,
Stood leaning on the granite shelf
Onegin, lost in meditation,
As once a bard described himself.[17]
And all is calm save for the trailing
Calls of a lonely watchman hailing
Another, and the distant sound
Of cabs that over pavements pound;
A lonely boat, its paddles weaving,
Was on the slumbering river borne;
And wayward singing, and a horn
Bewitched our ears, the silence cleaving . . .
Yet, 'mid nocturnal reveling
Torquato's octaves[18] sweeter sing!

I. 49

O waters of the Adriatic,
O Brenta! I shall see you, know
Your witching voice and be ecstatic
With inspiration's quickened flow!
To Phoebus' children consecrated,
By Albion's haughty lyre[19] translated,
It was my own and sang through me.
The nights of golden Italy,
On their delights I shall be gloating
At will; with a Venetian girl,
Her tongue now silent, now apurl,
In secret gondola be floating;
And in her arms my lips will strain
For Petrarch's and for love's refrain.

I. 50

When strikes my liberation's hour?
It's time, it's time—I bid it hail;
I pace the shore, the sky I scour
And beckon to each passing sail.[20]
Storm-canopied, wave-tossed in motion
On boundless highroads of the ocean,
When do I win unbounded reach?
It's time to leave the tedious beach
That damps my spirit, to be flying
Where torrid southern blazes char
My own, my native Africa,[21]
There of dank Russia to be sighing,
Where once I loved, where now I weep,
And where my heart is buried deep.

I. 51

My friend Onegin had decided
On foreign travel with me soon;
But presently we were divided
By destiny for many a moon.
His father's days just then had ended,
And promptly on Eugene descended
The moneylenders' hungry breed;
Each with his story and his deed.
Eugene, who hated litigation,
Accepting graciously his fate,
Made over the defunct estate
With no great sense of deprivation;
Perhaps he had an inkling, too,
That his old uncle's death was due.

I. 52

And as he had anticipated,
His uncle's steward soon sent news
That the old man was quite prostrated
And wished to say his last adieus.
In answer to the grievous tiding,
By rapid stage Eugene came riding
Posthaste to honor his behest;
Prepared, in view of the bequest,
For boredom, sighs, and simulation,
And stifling yawns well in advance
(With this I opened my romance):
But when he reached his destination,
His uncle lay on his last berth,
Due to be rendered unto earth.

I. 53

He found the manor full of mourners,
Connections dear and not so dear,
Who had converged there from all corners;
All funeral fans, it would appear.
They laid to rest the late lamented,
Then, dined and wined and well-contented,
The priest and guests left one by one,
Gravely, as from a job well done.
There was Eugene, a landed squire,
Of forests, waters, mills galore
The sovereign lord—he who before
Had been a scamp and outlaw dire—
And pleased to see his life's stale plot
Exchanged for—well, no matter what.

I. 54

Two days the solitary meadows
Retained for him their novel look,
The leafy groves with cooling shadows
And the sedately murmuring brook;
Next day he did not take the trouble
To glance at coppice, hill, and stubble,
Then they brought on a sleepy mood,
And he was ready to conclude:
Spleen does not spare the landed gentry,
It needs no palaces or streets,
No cards or balls or rhymed conceits.
Spleen hovered near him like a sentry
And haunted all his waking life
Like a shadow, or a faithful wife.

I. 55

I'm made to live in some still shire,
I thrive in rural quietude:
'Mid silence, bolder is the lyre,
More vivid the creative mood.
On simple pastimes bent, I wander
By the deserted lakeside yonder,
Dolce far niente is my code;
And each succeeding dawn can bode
But hours of freedom sweetly wasted.
I read a little, sleep a lot
And chase the phantom Glory not.
In years gone by, have I not tasted
In shadowed idleness like this
My most unclouded days of bliss?

I. 56

Wild blossoms, love, the country, leisure,
Green meadows—there is all my heart;
Once more I point it out with pleasure:
Eugene and I are souls apart.
I say this lest some sneering reader
Or any God-forsaken breeder
Of heinous libels should appear,
Profess to see my portrait here
And circulate the wicked fable
That I walk in my hero's dress,
Like Byron, bard of haughtiness,
As though we were by now unable
On any subject to intone
A song, but on ourselves alone.

I. 57

All poets—while I'm on these subjects—
Are given to daydreaming love;
My soul, too, harbored charming objects
Whom I at times have daydreamed of,
And kept an image of their features;
The Muse breathed life into these creatures,
Then I could safely serenade
Both my ideal, the mountain maid,
And the Salgir's fair slaves admire.[22]
These days I often listen to
A certain question, friends, from you:
"For whom, then, languishes your lyre?
Among the maiden's jealous throng,
To whom do you inscribe your song?"

I. 58

"Whose gazes, kindling inspiration,
Have recompensed from melting eyes
Your meditative incantation?
Whom did your verse immortalize?"
Why, nobody, my friends, I swear it!
Love's mindless anguish, should I bear it
Once more with no reward at all?
Blest he who in its throes could fall
Into a rhyming fit, thus double
Parnassus' sacred frenzy, sing,
In Petrarch's footsteps following,
And not just ease the heart's deep trouble
But earn a famous name to boot:
While I, in love, was deaf and mute.

I. 59

The Muse appeared, past Love's intrusion,
It cleared the mind in darkness bound,
And free once more, I seek the fusion
Of feeling, dream, and magic sound.
I write—no heartache stays my fingers,
The wayward pen no longer lingers
To trace near verse left incomplete
Vignettes of female heads and feet;
Those ashes will not be rekindled;
I grieve still, but I weep no more;
Soon, soon all marks the tempest wore
Into my soul will quite have dwindled:
And then—why then I'll write a song
Some five-and-twenty cantos long.

I. 60

I've thought about the hero's label
And on what lines the plot should run;
Meanwhile, it seems, my present fable
Has grown as far as Chapter One.
I have gone over it severely,
And contradictions there are clearly
Galore, but I will let them go,
Pay censorship its due, and throw
Imagination's newborn baby,
My labor's fruit with all its flaws
To the reviewers' greedy jaws:
To the Nevá, then, child, and maybe
You'll earn me the rewards of fame:
Distorted judgments, noise, and blame!

Kishinyov, Odessa,
October 22, 1823.

Notes

1. The dedication is addressed to Pushkin's publisher-friend, P. A. Pletnyov.

2. The original here alludes neatly but untranslatably to the well-known introductory line of one of Ivan Krylov's fables: "An ass of most respectable convictions . . ."

3. This is addressed to the readers of Pushkin's first major work in print, the mock-heroic fairy tale in verse, *Ruslan and Lyudmila* (1820).

4. A saucy reference to Pushkin's penal transfer from the northern capital (where Nevá flows) for his mildly subversive poems and mordant epigrams. Pushkin notes here: "Written in Bessarabia."

5. A favorite Pushkinian term for poetry.

6. Numbers in parentheses, here and elsewhere, indicate stanzas omitted by the author. Partially omitted stanzas will be indicated by ellipses (. . .).

7. "Hat à la Bolivar" (Pushkin's note).

8. "Well-known restaurateur" (Pushkin's note).

9. This name of a friend of Pushkin's, omitted or bracketed in many editions, is found in his manuscript.

10. The "Comet's vintage" is a champagne of the year 1811, memorable also for a comet.

11. This stanza celebrates the glories of the maturing Russian drama and ballet of the late eighteenth century, which had begun in close imitation of the French classics of Corneille, Racine, and Molière, but were then finding more truly Russian themes and accents. Of the dramatists mentioned, D. I. Fonvízin (1745–92) was a gifted satirist of manners and morals; Y. B. Knyazhnin (1742–91), V. A. Ozerov (1770–1816), and P. A. Katenin (1792–1853) represent French-inspired tragedy in various stages; A. A. Shakhovskoy (1777–1846) was a prolific writer of comedies. Charles-Louis Didelot (1767–1837) was a French balletmaster and choreographer associated with the early development of the Russian ballet. Semyonova was a Shakespearean actress prominent as the heroine in many of Ozerov's dramas.

12. One of Didelot's most famous ballerinas, celebrated in the 1820's for both her art and her beauty.

13. Pushkin explains this little aside by quoting a passage from Rousseau's *Confessions*, where Rousseau relates his encounter with Frédéric-Melchior Grimm, the Parisian critic and encyclopedist, correspondent of Catherine II.

14. The editor Tomashevsky's accepted insertion on MS evi-

dence for the name omitted here by Pushkin. Chadayev or Chaadayev was a friend of Pushkin's and was internationally noted for his elegance of dress and manners.

15. Boston, a four-handed card game developed from whist, said to have been invented by officers of the French fleet in Boston bay at the time of the British siege in 1775. Being faster-scoring and more of a game of chance than stodgy whist, it enjoyed a great vogue in French society by the turn of the century, and from there was soon introduced into fashionable Russian circles, who, of course, spoke French and used the French pronunciation of the game's name, rhyming with *salon*.

16. Pushkin heightened the effect of this elegant assault by annotating it with a wide-eyed explanation: "All of this ironical stanza is but a subtle compliment to our fair compatriots. Thus Boileau renders homage to Louis XIV in the guise of criticism. Our ladies combine enlightenment with amiability and strict moral purity with that oriental charm which so captivated Mme. de Stael. (See *Dix Années d'exil.*)"

17. Pushkin here quotes a quatrain from A. N. Muravyov's pseudo-archaic poem *To the Goddess of the Neva:* "Rapt in ecstasy, the singer, Hearkening the kindly Elf, Sees that sleepless he will linger, Leaning on the granite shelf."

18. The octave or double quatrain, *ottava rima,* used by Torquato Tasso in *Jerusalem Delivered*.

19. Allusion to Byron.

20. "Written at Odessa" (Pushkin's note). This was the last stage of his Southern "exile," 1823–24.

21. "The author, on his mother's side, is of African descent. His great-grandfather, Abram Petrovich Hannibal, was abducted at the age of eight from the shores of Africa and taken to Constantinople. The Russian envoy rescued him and sent him as a gift to Peter the Great, who had him christened at Wilno, standing godfather to him. . . ." Thus begins a lengthy note by Pushkin, sketching the colorful and distinguished career of his Ethiopian or Moorish ancestor and promising a complete biography in due course. He later undertook this work which, though unfinished, is an impressive sample of his historical scholarship and style. Pushkin was sometimes nicknamed "the African" for his whimsical emphasis on his exotic descent.

22. This refers to the heroines of two of Pushkin's just-published narrative poems, *The Prisoner of the Caucasus* and *The Fountain of Bakhchisaray*. The Salgir is the stream which waters Bakhchisaray (Bahçesaray in Turkish = "garden palace").

Chapter
Two

O rus! ...

HORACE

O Russia!

II. 1

The manor where Onegin fretted
Was so enchanting a retreat,
No simple soul would have regretted
Exile so pastoral and sweet:
The hall, well sheltered from intrusion
Of world and wind, stood in seclusion
Upon a stream-bank; and away
There stretched a shimmering array
Of meads and cornfields gold-brocaded,
And hamlets winked; across the grass
A wandering herd would slowly pass;
And leafy clusters densely shaded
The park, far-rambling and unkempt,
Where pensive dryads dwelt and dreamt.

II. 2

The hall was built on unpretentious
But solid lines, such as befit
The plain good taste and conscientious
Design of timeless mother-wit.
Room after room with lofty ceiling,
A tapestried *salon,* revealing
Ancestral portraits hung in file
And stoves, of many-colored tile.
All this has now been superseded,
Exactly why, I never learned;
But where Onegin was concerned,
In any case it went unheeded,
Because he yawned with equal gloom
In any style of drawing room.

II. 3

For his own use Eugene selected
The room where till his late demise
The laird had cursed his cook, inspected
The same old view, and swatted flies.
Couch, cupboards, table, all betoken
A simple taste; the floor is oaken,
Nowhere the faintest trace of ink,
The cupboards, opened to a chink,
Show batteries of homemade brandy
Some demijohns of applejack,
A twenty-year-old almanac
And an account book lying handy.
The busy squire had had no mind
For books of any other kind.

II. 4

Bored in his lordly isolation,
Just to relieve the daily norm,
Eugene at first found occupation
In bold agrarian reform.
The backwood wiseacre commuted
The harsh *corvée* and instituted
A quitrent system in its stead;
The serf called blessings on his head.
Whereat his thrifty neighbor, highly
Incensed, swelled in his nook and fought
The wicked and expensive thought;
Another only snickered slyly,
And one and all they set him down
As a subversive kind of clown.

II. 5

At first the neighbors started calling;
But when he kept by the back stoop,
Their visits artfully forestalling,
A Cossack cob (to fly the coop
When rumbles of a homely coach
First warned him of a guest's approach),
Such conduct struck them as ill bred,
And all the County cut him dead.
"Our neighbor is uncouth; he's crazy;
A freemason; he only drinks
Red wine in tumblers; never thinks
To kiss a lady's hand—too lazy;
It's 'yes' and 'no,' no 'ma'am' or 'sir.' "
In this indictment all concur.

II. 6

Just at this time the County sighted
One more young landlord, come to seek
His nearby manor, who invited
An equally severe critique.
Vladimir Lensky, in the flower
Of youthful looks and lyric power,
And impregnated to the core
With Göttingen and Kantian lore.
From German mists the poet-errant
Brought Teuton wisdom's clouded brew,
Dreams of a libertarian hue,
A spirit fiery, though aberrant,
Relentlessly impassioned speech,
And raven locks of shoulder reach.

II. 7

Not yet by worldly traffic hardened
Or by its chill corruption seared,
His soul still knew how to be ardent,
By maidens charmed, by friendship cheered.
Dear ignoramus in the science
Of life, hope was his fond reliance;
Across his mind the world still drew
Its web of glitter and ado;
With rosy dreams he would belittle
His spirit's dubious surmise;
The goal of life was to his eyes
A species of alluring riddle;
On it he exercised his mind
And nameless marvels there divined.

II. 8

He knew that fate had designated
A kindred soul for him alone,
Which, pining day and night, awaited
The longed-for union with his own;
That loyal friends and benefactors
Yearned for the blood of his detractors
And would not flinch from ball and chain
To keep his honor free from stain;
That higher counsels had selected
For each his private hallowed friend:
A deathless bond which in the end
By its own radiance undeflected
Would kindle us to shining worth
And scatter bliss upon the earth.

II. 9

Compassion, noble indignation,
High impulses' ingenuous urge,
Ambition's joyous agitation
Stirred in his soul an early surge;
Instinct with Goethe's, Schiller's fire,
He roamed creation with his lyre,
And in their poetry's domains
The blood was fired in his veins.
Nor, lucky fellow, did he ever
Put the exalted Muse to shame:
From his proud harp there never came
Aught but exalted feelings, never
Worse than a dreamy maiden's plea
Or praise of grave simplicity.

II. 10

Of love he sang, love's service choosing,
And limpid was his simple tune
As ever artless maiden's musing,
As babes aslumber, as the Moon
In heaven's tranquil regions shining,
Goddess of secrets and sweet pining;
He sang of partings, mists afar,
Of sorrow, of *je ne sais quoi*:
Romantic roses, distant islands
He used to sing of, where for years
He poured a generous toll of tears
Into the soothing lap of silence;
He mourned the wilt of life's young green
When he had almost turned eighteen.

II. 11

But for Eugene, here in the shires
His talents must have gone to waste;
The socials of the neighboring squires
Were little suited to his taste.
He shunned their rumbling congregations;
Their commonsensical orations
Of haylofts filled and wine laid in,
Of cattle, kennel, kith and kin
Were hardly such as to inspire
Or captivate with worldly wit,
With depth of feeling, exquisite
Discernment, or poetic fire;
But their dear wives' colloquial tone
Was far less highbrow than their own.

II. 12

The well-to-do "half-Russian neighbor,"
Good-looking, too, became fair game;
Much ingenuity and labor
Was spent by many a watchful dame
With daughters in whose paths to thrust him:
Such is the standing rural custom.
They chance to work in something light
About the bachelor's dreary plight
The moment he appears, and fluting
Him in where Dunya pours his cup,
They hiss to her: "Dunya, sit up!"
And then they even bring her lute in,
On which, ye gods, she starts to strum:
"Into my golden chamber come!"

II. 13

But Lensky, pardonably leery
Of signing a connubial lien,
Instead bestirred himself sincerely
To seek acquaintance with Eugene.
They met—none more unlike created,
Like wave and cliff absurdly mated,
Like ice and flame, or verse and prose.
Their alien ways at first impose
Constraint, but soon each finds the other's
Society a pleasant need;
They meet for daily rides; indeed
They soon are closer than two brothers.
Thus friends are made (I'm guilty, too)
For lack of something else to do.

II. 14

Today, among us would-be heroes
Such friendship, too, is dead, one shelves
All sentiment; we count as zeros
All other men except ourselves.
The world's Napoleons bemuse us:
Mankind, we think, is there to use as
So many million biped tools,
And feelings are for cranks and fools.
Eugene, endowed with more perception
Than many, knew and felt contempt
For men at large, but did exempt
A few (no rule without exception):
Their feelings, as beyond reproof,
He honored—though himself aloof.

II. 15

The poet's fiery effusions
Eugene met with a smiling glance,
The judgments riddled with delusions,
And the habitual look of trance—
All this to him seemed strange and novel;
But he was careful not to cavil,
Or check the flow with caustic curb,
And mused: Who am I to disturb
This state of blissful, brief infection?
Its spell will pass without my help;
Meanwhile, allow the dear young whelp
To glory in the world's perfection;
We must forgive youth's fever blaze
Both youthful heat and youthful craze.

II. 16

All subjects led to disputations
Between them and engendered thought;
The covenants of ancient nations,
The useful works by science wrought;
And Good and Evil, time-worn errors,
The great Beyond's mysterious terrors,
And Destiny and Life in turn
Engaged their serious concern.
Meantimes the poet, with the fulgence
Of his own phrases all ablaze,
Read fragments from the northern lays,
The while Onegin with indulgence,
Though he but little understood,
Took in intently what he could.

II. 17

More often, though, our friends debated
The passions in their wilderness;
From their harsh sway now liberated,
Onegin could not but confess
To some regretful animation:
Blest he who knew their agitation
And issued from it scarred but free,
Who never knew them, twice blest he,
And who could slake desire with parting,
Hate with abuse—what if he tends
To yawn alike at wife and friends,
With jealous anguish never smarting,
And his ancestral ducats guards
From the insidious deuce of cards.

II. 18

When we have rallied to the standard
Of a well-tempered quietude,
And blazing passions have been rendered
Absurd, their afterglow subdued,
Their lawless gusts and their belated
Last echoes finally abated—
Not without cost at peace again,
We like to listen now and then
To alien passion's rage and seething,
And feel its clamor at our heart;
We play the battered veteran's part
Who strains to listen, barely breathing,
To exploits of heroic youth,
Forgotten in his humble booth.

II. 19

For its part, adolescent fire
Cannot be secret or deceive;
Rejoicing, sadness, love, or ire,
They all are worn upon the sleeve.
Onegin, invalid of passion,
Would listen with a grave expression
As Lensky, eager to impart
What moved him, opened wide his heart.
His inmost hoard of artless feeling
Did he confidingly unveil;
His youthful love's ingenuous tale
Onegin was not long unsealing;
A most affecting story, true,
To us, however, far from new.

II. 20

He loved—ah, worshiped—in a fashion
Unheard of now: such fervid zeal
As but the mind, consumed with passion,
Of poets still is doomed to feel.
With but a sole desire swooning
One dream's relentless importuning,
A single ever-present grief.
Not sobering distance brought relief,
Not numbing years of separation,
Not riotous pleasure, learning's balm,
No alien beauty's perfumed arm,
Nor yet the Muse's consolation
Contrived to alter or compose
The soul ablaze with maiden glows.

II. 21

While half a boy yet (he recited),
Before love's agonizing stir,
He'd watched the child at play, delighted,
And felt his heart go out to her.
In sheltered groves, across the heather,
They used to sport and roam together,
Predestined for the marriage bond
By both their fathers—neighbors fond.
In her retreat, in peaceful shadow
She blossomed in her parents' view,
In charming innocence she grew
Like the shy lily of the meadow,
Unknown in her secluded lea
To butterfly and bumblebee.

II. 22

It was her image that had fired
His youthful fervor's virgin dream,
The thought of her which had inspired
The reed pipe's plaintive virgin theme.
Farewell, O golden time of frolic!
In sylvan groves the melancholic
Found in secluded silence boon
And worshiped Night, and Stars, and Moon—
The moon, celestial luminary,
To whom we, too, our toll have paid
Of many a twilight promenade
And weeping, hidden heartache's parry . . .
But lately we have seen in her
But one more lantern's tarnished blur.

II. 23

Gay as the morning sky, compliant
And modest ever like the dove,
Pure-minded like the Muse's client,
Dear as the kiss of youthful love,
All flaxen-ringleted and smiling,
Celestial blue of eyes, beguiling
By grace of movement, form, and voice,
Thus Olga . . . Novels (take your choice)
All paint the type to satisfaction:
She's an engaging little elf.
I once was fond of her myself,
But now she bores me to distraction.
Straight to her elder sister then,
Dear reader, let me turn my pen.

II. 24

Tatyana was her name . . . I grovel
That with such humble name I dare
To consecrate a tender novel.[1]
And yet, I ask you, is it fair
To sneer at it? It's full-toned, pleasant,
What if it's fragrant with a peasant
Antiqueness, if it does recall
The servant quarters? We must all
Confess, in names we have forsaken
Good taste—and elsewhere, too, it's weak
(Of verse I will not even speak);
Enlightenment just hasn't taken
Where we're concerned, for ever since
All we have learnt is how to mince.

II. 25

Tatyana, then . . . And I would mention
That no bright eyes, no rosy skin,
Were hers to help arouse attention
Such as her sister's looks would win.
Untamed, to wistful silence given,
Shy as a doe by hunters driven,
She seemed not born to them but found—
A stranger in the family round.
She'd never learnt to charm or soften
Her parents in a wheedling way;
A child herself, in children's play
She seldom wished to join, and often
Would spend long days of games and sport
By her own window, lost in thought.

II. 26

Imagination, which she relished,
From cradle days a dear resóurce,
Wrapped her in fancies which embellished
Her rustic life's unhurried course.
The delicately nurtured finger
Spurned needlework, nor would she linger,
Bent to embroidery hoops, to fine
Dull linen with a silk design.
A child at play before her forum
Of docile dolls (proof of the will
To dominate) learns by this drill
What makes the world go round—decorum,
And labors gravely to transfer
To them what Mama just taught *her*.

II. 27

But Tanya showed no inclination
To play with dolls when she was small,
Review with them in conversation
The gowns and gossip of the mall,
And childish mischief was not for her;
She rather thrilled to tales of horror,
Which of a somber winter night
Filled her with shuddering delight.
Again, when Nanny used to summon
All Olga's playmates, and had drawn
The girls around her on the lawn
To play a tag-game, it was common
To see her spurn the fun and noise,
A stranger to their giddy joys.

II. 28

Upon her balcony at dawning
She liked to bide the break of day,
When on the heavens' pallid awning
There fades the starry roundelay,
When earth's faint rim is set to glowing,
Aurora's herald breeze is blowing
And step by step the world turns light.
In wintertime, when darkling night
The hemisphere for longer covers,
And sunk in idle quietude,
Beneath a hazied moon subdued,
The languid Orient longer hovers—
Roused at accustomed time, she might
Begin the day by candlelight.

II. 29

But novels, which she early favored,
Replaced for her all other treats;
With rapturous delight she savored
Rousseau's and Richardson's conceits.
Her honest father, though old-fashioned,
Last century's child, grew not impassioned
About the harm that books might breed;
He, who was never known to read,
Regarded them as empty thrillers
And never thought to bring to light
Which secret volume dreamt at night
Beneath his little daughter's pillows.
His wife had had a crush herself
On Richardson—still on her shelf.

II. 30

The reason for her firm devotion
Was not the books she hadn't read,
Nor that from Lovelace her emotion
Had turned to Grandison instead.
No—they were brought to her attention
By Princess Ala's frequent mention
(Her cousin's) in her Moscow phase.
All this went back to bridal days,
When she had, much against her feeling,
Accepted Larin, while she pined
For quite another, to her mind
Incomparably more appealing:
This Grandison was fond of cards,
A fop, and sergeant of the Guards.

II. 31

In dress she was quite like her idol,
Stylish and exquisitely nice;
But presently they set her bridal
And never asked for her advice.
On purpose to appease her sorrow,
The wise young husband on the morrow
Left for the country, where her gloom,
Thrown as she was on God knows whom,
At first was measureless and tearful,
The marriage almost came to grief;
Then by and by she found relief
In management and grew quite cheerful.
Habit is Heaven's own redress;
It takes the place of happiness.[2]

II. 32

Thus habit soothed the grief that chafed her,
The ache that nothing could appease;
Then a great insight was vouchsafed her
That put her finally at ease:
Between the daily work and leisure
She soon contrived to take the measure
Of her good spouse and seize the reins;
This put an end to all her pains.
She went about her daily labors,
She labeled pickled-mushroom crocks,
She kept accounts, she shore off locks,[3]
Took Sabbath baths like all her neighbors,
Struck at the housemaids when so moved,
And never asked if he approved.

II. 33

Till then, her debutante demeanor
Meant album lines in heartsblood scrawled,
Praskovya smartened to Paulina,
And speech melodiously drawled;
Tight hourglass corsets she affected,
Her "n"s were expertly ejected
A la française and through the nose;
But country life wore down this pose;
The album, stays, Princess Alina,
The notebook full of feeling verse
Receded in her mind; the terse
Akulka ousted smart Celina;
At last she took to coming down
In cap and quilted dressing-gown.

II. 34

Her honest husband loved her dearly,
In her affairs he did not probe,
In all things trusted her sincerely,
And came to dinner in his robe.
His life maintained an even tenor:
Twilight might gather at the manor
Of neighbors a familiar troupe;
A friendly and informal group
Who grumbled, aired the latest scandals,
Enjoyed a laugh at this or that;
The shadows lengthened while they sat,
And Olga went to light the candles,
For supper is about to start,
And then comes bed. The guests depart.

II. 35

Their peaceful life was firmly grounded
In the dear ways of yesteryear,
And Russian *bliny* fair abounded
When the fat Shrovetide spread its cheer.
Two weeks a year they gave to fasting,
Were fond of games and fortune-casting,
Of roundelay and carrousel;
At Trinity, when peasants tell
Their beads and nod at morning prayer,
They dropped three tears upon the toll
Of lovage due a dear one's soul;
Their *kvas* they needed like fresh air,
And at their table guests were served
In order as their rank deserved.

II. 36

So they grew old like other mortals.
At last a final mansion drew
Asunder its sepulchral portals
Before the husband, wreathed anew.
Near dinnertime he died, contented,
By friends and neighbors much lamented,
By children, wife, and all his clan
More truly mourned than many a man.
He was a simple, kindly *barin,*
And where his earthly remnant rests,
A graven headstone thus attests:
"A humble sinner, Dmitri Larin,
God's servitor and brigadier,
Found peace beneath this marble here."

II. 37

To his ancestral hall returning,
Vladimir Lensky sought the plot
Of his old neighbor's last sojourning
And sighed in tribute to his lot.
And long he mourned for the departed:
"Poor Yorick!" quoth he, heavy-hearted,
"To think he nursed me in his day,
And on his lap I used to play
With his Ochákov[4] decoration!
He destined Olga's hand for me,
And often wondered, would he see
That day? . . ." In wistful agitation
He then and there indulged the urge
To pen for him a graveside dirge.

II. 38

There, too, in sorrowful remembrance
He hailed with epitaphs and tears
His parents' venerable remnants . . .
Alas—in furrows of the years
By an unfathomed dispensation
The seed of every generation
Strikes hurried root, and fruits, and fails,
And new seed rises in its trails . . .
Thus our own giddy wave goes rolling,
Swells high, and tosses foam, and raves,
And sweeps us to our forebears' graves.
Our own bell, friends, is tolling, tolling,
Our children's seed will come of age
And swiftly crowd us off the stage.

II. 39

Meanwhile drink deeply of life's essence,
Life's heady draught, enjoy it, friends!
I've learnt its disenchanting lessons,
Nor will it grieve me when it ends;
No ghost can pry my lids asunder;
Only at times a distant wonder
Has power yet to stir my heart:
It would be bitter if my part
On this brief stage would not leave on it
The faintest trace. I live and write
Not for applause; my dismal plight,
Let it but fuel the blazing sonnet,
One note that like a faithful friend
Bespeaks my name beyond the end.

II. 40

And then, who knows, that single trophy,
By Fate preserved, some heart will sway;
On Lethe's sleepy stream the strophe
I wrought will not be borne away;
Perhaps (sweet solace to the singer!)
Some oaf unborn will point his finger
At my famed likeness and declare:
There was a poet now for fair!
To thee my humble thanks I render,
Heir of Aonia's placid strains,
And thee, whose memory retains
My fleeting rhymes, whose hand is tender.
And not without indulgence strays
To the old codger's plaster bays!

Odessa,
December 8, 1823.

Notes

1. "The sweetest-sounding Greek names, such as Agathon, Philat, Theodora, Thekla, are used among us only by the common people" (Pushkin's note).

2. Pushkin here quotes Chateaubriand's remark: *"Si j'avois la folie de croire encore au bonheur, je le chercherois dans l'habitude."*

3. Serfs designated by their masters for army service had a fore-lock shaved off.

4. Commemorates the capture of the Black Sea fortress of Ochakov in 1783.

Chapter
Three

Elle était fille, elle était amoureuse.

MALFILÂTRE

III. 1

"Where are you off to? Oh, you—poet!"
"Good-by, Eugene, it's time I went."
"There is no holding you, I know it;
But where, pray, are your evenings spent?"
"Why, at the Larins'." "How intriguing!
And yet, own up, it grows fatiguing
To sit there, killing time, no doubt?"
"Of course not." "I can't make you out.
I know the place without inspection:
You find (correct me if you can)
A simplehearted Russian clan
That treats a guest to great affection,
Preserves, and everlasting yarns
Of rain and flax and cattle barns. . . ."

III. 2

"And if they were like that, what of it?"
"Dear chap, it simply is a bore."
"What if I see no charm or profit
In worldly glamour, setting store
By homefolk . . . ?" "There's an eclogue for you!
Spare me the rest, friend, I implore you.
I see you have made up your mind.
Good night! Yet, after all, I find
Your Phyllis strangely interesting,
Who stirs your heart and pen so much—
Transports, and rhymes, and tears and such—
Come, introduce me!" "You are jesting."
"No!" "Very well, then." "When?" "Tonight;
They will receive us with delight."

III. 3

"Let's go."
          The nimble carriage races;
They make their entrance, and are met
With all the heavy-handed graces
Of a time-honored etiquette.
We know the hospitable ritual:
Small bowls of jam and the habitual
Bilberry-water jug turn up
Upon an oilcloth tabletop,
Then eating never ends till day does;
Arms snugly folded, half a score
Of servant maidens crowd the door
To marvel at the strange invaders,
And in the yard a jury stands
To judge their horses' points and hands.[1]

III. 4

In full career the coach is veering,
Bound homeward by the shortest way.
Let us keep silent, overhearing
What our heroes have to say:
"Yawning, Eugene? So dull a visit?"
"Oh, just a habit, Lensky." "Is it?
You seem more bored than ever." "No,
About the same. It's darkening, though;
Speed up, Andryushka, hurry, will you?
A dreary stretch, this! By the way,
Old Larina is sweet, I'd say,
Though scarcely anything to thrill you,
And that bilberry elixir
May rise to haunt me yet, I fear.

III. 5

"But tell me—which one was Tatyana?"
"Why, she who with an absent air,
Remote and wistful like Svetlana,[2]
Came in and took the window chair."
"Yet it's the younger you admire?"
"Why not?" "Your Olga's face lacks fire;
If I wrote poetry like you,
I'd choose the elder. Like your true
Van Dyck Madonna, Olga's blended
Of peach and cream, as round and soft
As that insipid moon aloft
On that insipid dome suspended."
His friend made some retort, and then
The whole way back spoke not again.

III. 6

Meanwhile, of course, Onegin's calling
At Squire Larin's house was bound
To launch a theme that proved enthralling
To friend and neighbor all around.
Conjecture followed on conjecture,
Sly jest bred guesswork, rumor, lecture,
They gossiped and romanced away
Till Tanya had a fiancé:
The wedding vows, it next transpired,
Were settled on, the only thing
To wait for was the style of ring
That fashion nowadays required.
Of Lensky, people in the know
Had made a bridegroom long ago.

III. 7

Cross at these rumors, in some measure
Tatyana was dismayed to find
She pondered them with secret pleasure
And could not ban them from her mind;
As seed into the furrow flowing
Awakes to Spring's rekindled glowing,
Dreams sank upon her from above,
And presently she was in love.
Long since, her young imagination,
Enflamed in tender, languored mood,
Had yearned for the celestial food,
Long had a throbbing agitation
In vain sought in her bosom room;
Heart thirsting for . . . it knew not whom

III. 8

Now found him . . . And in wonder gazing,
She could but whisper—So it's he!
Alas! Henceforth her days and blazing
Lone-sleeping nights are never free
Of him: all things and every hour
Bespeak him with a magic power.
The looks of worried maids, the sound
Of kind solicitude she found
In equal measure irritating.
When guests came, absent and distressed
She scarcely answered when addressed,
Resentful of their leisured prating,
The unexpected calls they paid,
And once arrived, how long they stayed.

III. 9

With what unwonted fascination
She now devours *romans d'amour,*
With what a rapturous elation
Yields to their treacherous allure!
Creative fancy's vivid creatures
Lend their imaginary features—
He who adored Julie Wolmar,
Malek-Adhel, and de Linar,[3]
Young Werther, by his passion rended,
And Grandison, the demigod
Who causes you and me to nod—
Our tender dreamer saw them blended
Into a single essence warm,
Embodied in Onegin's form.

III. 10

Her fancy-fed imagination
Casts her in turn as heroine
Of every favorite creation,
Julie, Clarissa, or Delphine.[4]
Insidious book in hand, she wanders
Alone in forest hush and ponders
To seek and find in it her own
Mute blaze, her dreams, her heartstrings' tone;
She sighs, and in herself discovers
Another's glow, another's smart,
Abstractedly recites by heart
Fond messages to borrowed lovers . . .
But hers, whatever type you guessed,
Was not a Grandison, at best.

III. 11

Time was when fervent author-teachers,
Their pens attuned to grace and worth,
Gave their protagonists the features
Of bright perfection come to earth.
The cherished objects, hunted ever
By wicked persecution, clever
And highly strung bestrode their books,
Abetted by attractive looks.
With purest passion all afire,
The noble hero seemed to yearn
For sacrifice at every turn,
And halfway through the final quire
Vice was invariably scored
And Virtue reaped its due reward.

III. 12

But minds are all unhinged at present,
True worth is boring to this age;
Outside of novels, vice seems pleasant,
And in them, it is all the rage.
The British Muse's eerie ravings
Haunt Missie in her sleep; her cravings
Are all for brooding vampires now,
Or wandering Melmoth, dark of brow,
Or doomed Ahasverus who drifted
From land to land, or bold Corsair,
Or Sbogar with his secret air.[5]
Lord Byron's apt conceits have lifted
Bleak egoism up to shine
In the Romantic's gloomy shrine.

III. 13

This surely, friends, defies all reason!
Perhaps, who knows, a novel curse
Will fall on me in proper season,
I shall no longer speak in verse,
But placid prosy channels follow
And brave the anger of Apollo;
Then the old-fashioned novel's cheers
Shall occupy my waning years.
The secret miscreant's perdition,
His terrors, shall be left untold,
But soberly I will unfold
Old Russia's family tradition;
Young love's intoxicating dreams,
Our ancient ways, shall be my themes.

III. 14

I shall recount the simple speeches
Of Dad and Granddad in my book,
The children's trysts by ancient beeches,
Or on the borders of a brook;
The ravages of jealous torment,
Partings, reunion tears, long dormant
I shall stir up once more, and then
In marriage soothe them down again . . .
The language of impassioned pining
Will I renew, and love's reply,
The like of which in days gone by
Came to me as I lay reclining
At a dear beauty's feet, bemused,
And which of late I have not used.

III. 15

Tatyana, Tanya, whom I cherish!
My tears now flow with yours; the sands
Are running out, and you must perish
At our modish tyrant's hands.
But not at once—let hope engender
Its heedless bliss, while you surrender
To life's endearments for a while;
Oblivious to its tender guile
You sip the poison draught of yearning,
Dreams haunt you everywhere you go,
At every turning you foreknow
The chance encounter, keep discerning
At every step, at every glance
Your fateful tempter's countenance.

III. 16

Love's languorous unease assails her,
She walks into the park to brood,
But limbs grow leaden, vision fails her,
Beset by sudden lassitude;
Her heart is full to overflowing,
Her cheeks with ambient blushes glowing,
Her breath halts on the lip and dies,
Her ears a-murmur, dazed her eyes . . .
Night falls; the guardian moon commences
Her round across the starry cove,
The nightingale in misty grove
Intones its sonorous cadenzas.
Tatyana, wakeful in the gloom,
Confides to Nanny in her room:

III. 17

"Oh, Nanny, it's too close for sleeping!
Let in some air, and sit with me."
"What is it, child?" "I feel like weeping . . .
Let's talk of things that used to be."
"But what, dear? Once, when I was sprier,
My mind held all you might desire
Of olden tales, some true, some not,
Of sprites and maids . . . but I forgot;
Now my old head can't think of any,
My Tanya, all is dim. Alas,
I'm coming to a sorry pass,
I get so muddled . . ." "Tell me, Nanny,
When you were young, try to recall,
You never were in love at all?"

III. 18

"Why, Tanya, hush! We did not bother
With suchlike notions in my day;
God rest her soul, my husband's mother
She would have nagged my life away."
"Well, how then did you marry, Nyanya?"
"God willed it, likely, child . . . My Vanya
Was younger than I was, dear pet;
I hadn't fourteen summers yet.
The broker-woman came a-plying
Around my kin two weeks; I cried
When Dad, he blessed me for a bride.
Then they unwound my braids, and crying
In fear and trembling, I was led
By singing maidens to be wed.

III. 19

"And so, from home and kinfolk parted . . .
But you're not listening, my pet—"
"Oh, Nan, old Nan, I'm so downhearted,
I'm not myself, dear, all upset;
I feel like sobbing, crying, maybe . . ."
"You must be taken sick, my baby;
May Heaven keep you and preserve!
Say what you want, and let me serve . . .
I'll sprinkle Holy Water on you,
You're burning up with fever . . ." "No,
Not fever . . . I'm . . . in love, you know."
"May God have mercy, child, upon you!"
And the old nurse, in prayerful awe,
Crossed Tanya with her wasted claw.

III. 20

"I am in love," she muttered dourly
At the old crone. "My precious dove,
You're ailing, you are taken poorly."
"No, let me be, nurse; I'm in love."
And all the while the moon was shining
And in its fallow gleam outlining
Tatyana's cheek with sickly glare,
The loose profusion of her hair,
Her coursing tears, and looming plainer
Beside our youthful heroine,
Wrapped in her fleecy cloak of skin
The kerchiefed, silver-haired retainer.
And all lay in a dreamy swoon—
Beneath the old enchantress Moon.

III. 21

Afar Tatyana's spirit wandered,
As she sat gazing at the moon . . .
When there rose up in her unpondered
A thought . . . "I shall lie down quite soon;
You go—just one more favor do me,
Bring table, pen, and paper to me.
That's all." And in the hush of night
She sits alone, the moon for light,
And head in hand, begins inditing,
Eugene unceasingly in mind,
Her guileless maiden love, enshrined
In unpremeditated writing.
There—signed and folded is the note . . .
Child! Do you know to whom you wrote?

III. 22

With beauties have I been acquainted
As pure as winter and as kind,
Untouched, untempted, and untainted
Inviolate even to the mind;
I have admired their self-possession,
Their innate virtue and discretion,
And run for cover, I avow,
As if beholding at their brow
The dread inscription over Hades:
"Abandon hope who enter here."
To kindle feeling strikes with fear,
And to repel, delights these ladies.
On the Nevá's banks, I dare say
You have met vestals such as they.

III. 23

And others shine there, proudly wielding
Adherents to their service bent,
Themselves complacently unyielding
To passion's plea and blandishment.
And what was I amazed to witness?
When with a show of rigid fitness
They've driven bashful love away,
They lure it back into the fray
By a judicious use of kindness:
The words at any rate appear
At times less formal and severe—
And with impressionable blindness
The love-game's innocent recruit
Returns to the inane pursuit.

III. 24

How is Tatyana's failing greater?
That, sweetly ignorant of pose,
She proves no shrewd dissimulator
But trustful of the dream she chose?
Because she loves without concealing,
Obeys the urge of guileless feeling,
Her nature too confiding-swift,
Endowed by Heaven with the gift
A thousand fancies to engender,
With wits and will above her kind,
Originality of mind,
A heart inflammable and tender?
Would you not hesitate to scourge
The recklessness of passion's urge?

III. 25

A flirt allures with calculation,
Tatyana's love is his to keep,
Without reserve or hesitation,
As dear as children's and as deep.
She has not learnt to whisper: tarry—
With choicer bait to trap the quarry
The more securely in the net,
Designing here with hope to whet
Vainglory, there to leave suspended
The doubting heart, then stoke desire
To higher blaze with jealous fire,
Lest, ardor in fulfillment ended,
The cunning slave should entertain
A restless urge to slip his chain.

III. 26

I can foresee a complication:
My country's honor to defend,
I'll have to furnish a translation
Of Tanya's letter in the end.
She knew our language only barely,
Read Russian magazines but rarely;
In her own language she was slow
To make her meaning clear, and so
She wrote in French, be it admitted . . .
I cannot help it, it is true:
To speak milady's love, but few
Have thought our native language fitted,
Our haughty Russian hardly knows
How to adjust to postal prose.

III. 27

I know our girls are being lectured
To read in Russian. Bah, what next!
Can they conceivably be pictured
Engrossed in the *Right-Thinker*'s[6] text?
I call on my own kind, the poet,
To bear me out, for we all know it:
By those whom, for your sins, you chose
To woo with secret verse, by those
To whom your heart was dedicated,
The Russian language (which they all
Used ill and crudely, if at all)
Was it not sweetly violated?
And did not foreign speech appear
Familiar on their lips and dear?

III. 28

Send me, Almighty, I petition,
In porticoes or at a ball
No bonneted academician,
No seminarist in a yellow shawl!
No more than in red lips unsmiling
Can I find anything beguiling
In grammar-perfect Russian speech.
What purist magazines beseech,
A novel breed of belles may heed it
And bend us (for my life of sin)
To strict grammatic discipline,
Prescribing meter, too, where needed;
But I—what is all this to me?
I like things as they used to be.

III. 29

That nonchalantly careless drawling,
That sweetly mispronouncing tongue,
To me its purl is still enthralling
As once it was when I was young;
The Gallic touch, no use recanting,
To me will always be enchanting
As youthful sins when youth is gone,
As Bogdanóvich's verse[7] . . . Pass on,
Enough of this. There is the letter
Of my dear beauty to translate;
Too bad, but such is now my fate,
Though to beg off would have been better;
For Parny's pen,[8] his gentle grace,
These days have lost their honored place.

III. 30

O bard of feasts and languid sorrow,[9]
Would that you were still with me here,
I should have boldly sought to borrow
Your magic for a spell, my dear:
To see in your bewitching cadence
New-rendered my impassioned maiden's
Bizarre epistolary flight!
Where are you? Come: my prior right
I make it over to you gladly . . .
But, weaned his heart from human praise,
Amid portentous cliffs he strays
'Neath Finland's heaven low'ring sadly,
A lonesome wand'rer, and his soul
Does not perceive my grievous dole.

III. 31

What Tanya wrote is in my keeping,
I treasure it like Holy Writ;
I cannot read it without weeping
Nor ever read my fill of it.
Who, what, unsealed that fount of feeling,
With such unguarded grace revealing
(Naïve appeal of artless art)
Her unpremeditating heart,
Alike disarming and imprudent?
I cannot answer—anyhow,
Here is my weak translation now,
Life's pallid copy by a student,
Or *Freischütz* waveringly played
By pupils awkward and afraid.

Tatyana's Letter to Onegin

I write to you—what more is needed?
This said, have I not said enough?
And you are free now, I concede it,
To crush me with a chill rebuff.
Yet if one droplet may be pleaded
Of your compassion for my plight—
You will not cast me from your sight.
At first I would have sooner perished
Than spoken of it, and I claim
You never would have known my shame,
Could I have confidently cherished
Some hope that, though but once a week,
You'd call on us, I'd hear you speak,
Just hear your voice in friendly greeting,
Perhaps exchange a word with you,
Then ponder ever and anew
One thought—until another meeting.
But you are hard to meet, they say,

The rustic backwoods simply bore you,
And we don't shine in any way,
Have but a hearty welcome for you.
Why did you ever come to call?
In our remote and sleepy borough,
Not having known of you at all,
I would be spared this bitter sorrow.
I might in time—who knows, tomorrow—
Have stilled the soul's young urge and strife,
Have let my heart seek out another;
I would have been a loving mother
And a devoted, faithful wife.
Another! . . . No—my heart could never
Become another's here! Not mine,
A higher Will, once and forever
Must have decreed it—I am thine.

All my past life was but a token
Our faithful meeting to portend;
I know thou art by God bespoken
To have and hold me to the end. . . .
In dreams of mine you kept appearing
And, sight unseen, were dear to me,
Your gaze has worked its spell on me,
Your voice resounded in my hearing
So long . . . No phantom did I see!
I knew you well at first beholding,
My cheeks caught fire, my knees were folding,
I whispered to myself: It's he!
Am I not right—you used to cheer me,
Commune with me by mute caress
When I gave alms? Did you not hear me
Each time I prayed for someone near me
To soothe the stricken soul's distress?
And at those very moments, surely
'Twas your dear form I saw obscurely
Out of the limpid dusk appear
And softly lay your head beside me,

And none but you who seemed to guide me
With whispered words of love and cheer?
My angel then, my preservation,
Or the fell demon of temptation,
Which are you? Make my doubts depart;
All this, it may be, is misguided,
Delusion of a callow heart,
And Fate has otherwise decided . . .
But be it so! What is in store
For me is now in your safekeeping,
And your protection I implore
As though I stood before you weeping . . .
Consider: I am here alone,
And everyone about mistakes me,
My understanding, too, forsakes me,
In silence must I be undone.
I wait your word: One intimation
My hope to hearten and revive,
Or this oppressive dream to rive,
Alas, with earned humiliation!

I close—and dare not to reread
These lines, by shame and terror haunted. . . .
But let your honor for me plead,
To it I trust my fate undaunted. . . .

III. 32

Tatyana mingles sobs with sighing,
The letter in her hand is wrung,
The rosy-colored wafer drying
Unused upon her fevered tongue.
At length, the little head subsiding
Toward one side, her nightgown sliding
Off one fair shoulder, she remains . . .
And now the lunar radiance wanes
And fades away. The distant valley
Shines clearer through the mist, the stream
Is jeweled with a silver gleam
And horn notes sound the village rally;
At home they've long begun the day;
My Tanya's thoughts are miles away.

III. 33

Dawn steals upon Tatyana musing,
Still huddled over what she wrote;
And still her finger shrinks from using
Her graven seal upon the note.
But presently the door starts creaking,
White-haired Filípevna is peeking
Around it with the morning cup.
"It's time, my child, time to get up. . . .
What, ready? And me come to dress you!
That's what I call an early chick!
Here I was worried you were sick,
But you are well and blooming, bless you!
Your fretful night left not a trace,
Like poppy-blossom glows your face."

III. 34

"Oh, Nanny, may I ask a service?"
"My own, ask anything you choose."
"Don't think . . . it looks . . . I am so nervous!
You see, it is . . . just don't refuse!"
"Why, dearie, by the Saints I swear it!"
"Take this, then, let your grandson bear it,
This note, I mean, to, oh . . . you know,
Our neighbor . . . only, tell him so,
He mustn't breathe a word about it,
Nor let my name be mentioned, pray . . ."
"Where should he take it, did you say?
I missed your meaning, I don't doubt it.
Of neighbors there be scores about;
How would I pick the right one out?"

III. 35

"Come, can't you guess a little, Nanny?"
"I'm old, my heart, and not so spry
As once I was; oh, I was canny
Before age dulled me, I was sly,
My mistress' slightest word was heeded . . ."
"Oh, Nanny, none of this is needed,
What would I want your slyness for?
It's just a note, see, nothing more,
To send Onegin." "Aye, don't holler,
Just don't get angry now, my lamb,
You know how slow to guess I am. . . .
Why, once again you're changing color!"
"It's nothing, Nan, do as I say,
Just send your grandson over, pray."

III. 36

The day wore on without a token,
The second morning, too, went by;
Ghost-pale, Tatyana, having woken
At dawn, awaited his reply.
Then Olga's cavalier came riding.
"Tell me, where can your friend be hiding?"
The hostess tried to draw him out.
"He has forgotten us, no doubt."
Tatyana hotly flushed and shivered.
"He promised to be here today."
She presently heard Lensky say,
"Perhaps the post has been delivered."
At this Tatyana caught her breath
As if condemned to instant death.

III. 37

Dusk settled; on the table gleaming
The tea urn breathed its steady lisp,
The china pot atop it seeming
To perch upon a swirling wisp.
By Olga's fingers poured and blended,
Into the proffered cups descended
The fragrant brew in amber curves;
A boy was handing round preserves.
Tatyana, by the window pond'ring,
Breathed on the chilly pane, apart
And lost in thought; and there, dear heart,
Her dainty finger, idly wand'ring,
Upon the clouded window traced
An "E" and "O" all interlaced.

III. 38

And all the while her heart was aching,
Suffused with tears her languid gaze.
All of a sudden, hoofbeats! Quaking,
She strains . . . Yes, closer . . . it's a chaise,
Eugene! "Oh!" Like a shadow fleeting
Tatyana crossed the hall, retreating
Past landing, stairs, and courtyard, right
Into the park in headlong flight;
Without a backward glance, she rounded
The pleasance, bridgelets, formal lawn,
Pond-lane and grove, and like a fawn
Broke through the lilac screen and bounded
Through flower beds toward the bank,
And there, her bosom heaving, sank

III. 39

Upon a bench . . .

    "He's here! Whatever,
O Heaven! must Eugene have thought?"
All anguish, still she loathes to sever
The web of hope her mind has wrought.
While tremors shake her, blushes riot,
She dreads his footfall. . . . But all quiet
The garden dreams, save for the maids
A-chanting in the berry glades.
While picking berries, they had orders
To sing in unison, sly lips
Too busy for the furtive nips
That would despoil the teeming borders
Of Master's berries—shrewd decree
Of rustic ingenuity!

The Maidens' Song

Hearty lassies, beauties fair,
Darling sisters, playmates dear,
Weave your circles, lassies, lovelies,
Strolling, sporting, far and near,
Let it lilt, our little carol,
Artful weaving little song,
Lure him on, the lusty lad,
Waylay him with roundelays.
Liltingly we tempt the lad,
As we spy him from afar,
Scatter, saucies, scamper, dears,
Fend him off with cherry twigs,
Cherry branches, berry vines,
Ruby-clustered currant sprigs.
Teach him not to overhear
Wheeling, reeling little tunes,
Teach him not to hover near,
Spying on our maiden games.

III. 40

They pick and chant, but all unheeding
Tatyana hears the tuneful quest,
Intent to calm, but only feeding,
The pulsing tumult in her breast,
Intent her blushes to dissemble;
In vain—her heart is still atremble,
The flaming cheek no paler grows,
But brighter, ever brighter glows.
Just so the luckless moth will quiver
And thrill the iridescent wing,
Caught on a willful schoolboy's string;
Just so the autumn hare will shiver
As in a thicket far afield
It spies the huntsman half-concealed.

III. 41

At last she sighed and rose, forsaking
Her rustic bench, and had resumed
Her way, when of a sudden taking
A turn aside—before her loomed
Eugene in person, glances sparkling,
Portentous like a shadow darkling,
And she, as though by fire seared,
Shrank and stood rooted as he neared.
But by your leave, I feel unequal
Just now, dear friends, to adding more
To all that has been said before
And tell this chance encounter's sequel;
I need to rest and have some fun:
Some other time I'll get it done.

Odessa, Mikhailovskoye,
1824.

Notes

1. The last six lines of this stanza are omitted in most editions.

2. Svetlana, title heroine of a ballad by Pushkin's friend Zhukovsky, a poet of high rank and reputation.

3. "Julie Wolmar—*La Nouvelle Héloïse*. Malek-Adhel, hero of a mediocre novel by Mme. Cottin. Gustave de Linar, hero of a charming novella by Baroness Krüdener" (Pushkin's note).

4. Julie is the heroine of Rousseau's *La Nouvelle Héloïse*; Clarissa, the heroine of Richardson's *Clarissa Harlowe*; Delphine, the title heroine of Mme. de Staël's novel.

5. The romantic tale *The Vampire* (1819) by J. W. Polidori, popular in the 1820's, was based on a brief outline by Byron, hence often attributed to him—wrongly, as Pushkin points out in a note here. *Melmoth the Wanderer*, by C. R. Maturin, which appeared the next year (1820), also appealed to the romantic taste for adventure and outlandish horrors. Sbogar refers to the hero of Charles Nodier's story, *Jean Sbogar* (1818).

6. *The Right-Thinker* or *The Well-Intentioned* (*Blagonamerenny*) was a Moscow literary journal edited (somewhat haphazardly, as Pushkin remarks in a note) by A. E. Izmaylov.

7. I. F. Bogdanovich (1743–1803), a Ukrainian poet of Catherine's age, whose narrative poem *Dúshenka*, based on La Fontaine's *Psyché et Cupidon*, scored a lasting success.

8. E. D. D. de Parny (1753–1814), French poet of late classicism, whose elegies and graceful erotic verse strongly influenced the generation of Russian poets preceding Pushkin, and clearly affected his own early style also.

9. Pushkin here refers in a note to E. A. Baratynsky or Boratynsky (1800–44), a minor poet and friend of his, who was then in disgrace in Finland.

Chapter
Four

La morale est dans la nature des choses.

NECKER

(IV. 1–6)

IV. 7

The less we love her, the more surely
We stand to gain a woman's heart
And ruin her the more securely,
Ensnared by the seducer's art.
Coldblooded rakes once placed reliance
In brazen amatory science;
Forever blowing their own horn,
They lusted, holding love in scorn.
That worthy game has all the flavor
Of those old simians who won praise
From Granddad in the good old days;
But Lovelace now is out of favor
His fashion gone with the appeal
Of towering wig and scarlet heel.

IV. 8

Who is not bored beyond endurance
To turn one thing now thus, now so,
Seal with elaborate assurance
What all were sure of long ago?
Forever hear the same expressions,
Annihilating prepossessions
None held, or would be apt to hold,
But flappers under twelve years old?
Who is not sick of pleas, effusions,
Of threats and oaths, pretended scares,
Of jottings—seven-page affairs—
Of tears, rings, gossip, fond illusions,
Of moms and aunts who sit up late,
And jovial husbands hard to hate?

IV. 9

Just such were my Eugene's conclusions,
Who in his youth had known the sway
Of those tempestuous delusions,
Unbridled passions' helpless prey.
Life's soothing custom once implanted,
He now was by one thing enchanted,
Now disenchanted by the next,
By surfeit of desire vexed,
Vexed by success too fleet and trifling,
Perceiving, too, in storm and calm
The restive spirit's murmuring qualm,
Yet weariness in laughter stifling:
Eight years had he now squandered so
And lost life's freshest, finest glow.

IV. 10

Gone were the days when love bemused him,
He managed somehow, undismayed,
Consoled at once if belles refused him,
Glad to relax if they betrayed,
As he pursued them unenchanted,
He took a painless end for granted
And scarce recalled their love or spite.
Just so a seasoned player might
Arrive for whist, go into action,
And calmly at the end of play
Say his adieus and drive away
To sleep with perfect satisfaction,
And in the morning never know
Where in the evening he might go.

IV. 11

Yet when Tatyana's note was brought him,
Onegin was profoundly stirred:
The voice of maiden dreams besought him,
Sent fancies swarming, would be heard;
Tatyana's image rose before him
And, wan and sad, seemed to implore him;
A dream of sinless, sweet delight
Engrossed his spirit at the sight.
Perhaps that vision did engender
A flash of feelings long at bay;
But he resolved not to betray
A trusting spirit's pure surrender . . .
Now let us hasten to the park
Where Tanya met him in the dark.

IV. 12

A timeless moment both were quiet;
But then Eugene approached and said:
"You wrote me—pray, do not deny it.
Your letter showed me, as I read,
A loving, trustful soul, revealing
The fullness of its guiltless feelings.
Your candor makes you dear to me;
And let me own that it set free
Emotions long in mute abeyance,
Yet to approve would not be right;
Instead, permit me to recite
A plea as artless in conveyance;
Accept my own confession now,
And to your judgment I will bow."

IV. 13

"If my own character inclined me
To the familial hearth and house;
If Fate had pleasantly designed me
To be a father and a spouse;
Had ever snug domestication
But for one instant held temptation:
On finding you, I dare confide,
I should have sought no other bride.
I say it with no minstrel flourish:
My old ideal, no sooner known,
I should have claimed you for my own,
To cheer my mournful days and nourish,
Dear pledge of every grace and good,
And been as happy . . . as I could!

IV. 14

"By me such bliss will not be tasted,
My soul is strange to its delight;
On me your perfect gift is wasted,
I dare not claim it as my right.
I know (my conscience be your warrant),
Our married life would grow abhorrent
To both of us; however much
I loved, at habit's chilling touch
My heart would cool, and all your weeping
Would not be able to implore
It back, but just outrage it more.
What roses Hymen may be keeping
In store for us—you judge it well!—
And for what ages, who can tell?

IV. 15

"What in the world could be more arid
Than twosomes where the wretched wife
Pines for the worthless man she married,
Condemned to lead a lonely life;
While he, who knows her worth (yet never
Ceases to curse his lot) is ever
Monosyllabic, sullen, blue,
Annoyed, and coldly jealous, too?
And him you chose—for I'm no better—
When from your pure and ardent heart
You wrote me so devoid of art
And yet so childish-wise a letter!
Is this to be the sad estate
Assigned you by a savage Fate?

IV. 16

"Spent dreams, spent years there's no reliving,
I can't rejuvenate my soul. . . .
A brother's love is in my giving,
And, yes, perhaps a fonder toll.
Don't chafe at one last admonition:
Your age may render the transition
From dream to dream as light and brief
As a young tree renews its leaf
With each returning vernal season.
Thus doubtless Heaven has decreed.
You will love others . . . But you need
To temper tenderness with reason:
Men will not always spare you so,
And inexperience leads to woe."

IV. 17

Thus went Onegin's sermon. Quailing,
Tatyana listened to him preach;
From streaming tears her sight was failing,
She scarcely breathed, bereft of speech.
Thus on his arm, in numb depression
("Mechanically" runs the expression),
Tatyana was in silence led,
And dazedly hung the little head
As she went homeward by the garden.
They came together, and no move
Was made to carp or disapprove.
The country grants a happy pardon
To rustic liberties as wide
As ever Moscow's in her pride.

IV. 18

My reader, can you help bestowing
Praise on Eugene for the fine part
He played with stricken Tanya? Showing
Simple nobility of heart
Once more to be among his features,
Although his spiteful fellow creatures
Saw nothing in him but a cad.
What foes he had, what friends he had
(Same thing, perhaps, on close inspection)
Befouled him, each in his own way.
We all have enemies, I say,
But friends—the Lord grant us protection!
What friends they were to me, my friends!
They cannot lightly make amends.

IV. 19

How so? Just so. I've no intention
To nurse my brooding vain and wry:
Just in parentheses I mention,
There is no despicable lie
By curs in attics fabricated
And by the leisured mob inflated,
There's never a transparent sham
Or slimy gutter epigram
That your good friends (with smiling faces,
Without a sly or evil thought)
To decent people are not caught
Repeating in a hundred places;
And then they bridle with chagrin;
You see, they love you . . . like your kin!

IV. 20

Heigh ho . . . Sweet reader, let me question,
How is your family? All well?
If you don't mind the mere suggestion
And are at leisure, let me tell
The proper meaning of "relations."
Here goes, then, word and connotations:
Folk to be earnestly revered,
Deferred to, cosseted, and cheered;
At Christmas, thus decrees convention,
One goes to see them without fail
Or sends them greetings through the mail,
Just to be paid no more attention
For the remainder of the year . . .
A ripe old age God grant them here!

IV. 21

But then, the love of gentle beauties
Holds greater hope than kin or friend:
Your claim upon their tender duties
Runs uncontested to the end.
Of course. But Fashion's whiplash swishes,
But Nature, headstrong and capricious,
But People's ever-potent frown—
And the dear sex proves light as down.
What's more, the husband's sage opinion
Must ever from his helpmeet true
Receive its full and honest due;
And so our ever-faithful minion
Is in a flash enticed away:
Where Love is, Satan likes to play.

IV. 22

Whom to believe, then, whom to treasure,
Our sole resort and citadel,
Content our words and deeds to measure
Obsequiously by our own ell?
Who spreads no slander that defames us?
Who fondly coddles, never blames us?
Who takes our faults without a fuss?
Who never gets fed up with us?
O idle seeker, phantom-breeder,
Lest thwarted ever be your quest,
Love your own self, I would suggest,
Respected and deserving reader!
A worthy object: surely none
Could possibly be greater fun.

IV. 23

What was the outcome of that meeting?
Alas, it is not hard to guess:
Love's numb ache did not cease from eating
Into the heart that craved distress.
Far from it, poor Tatyana's burning
With but perverser glow of yearning
The more despairing to appease,
And from her pillow slumber flees;
Her health, life's melody and color,
Her smile, her virginal repose,
All this like empty chatter goes
To waste, dear Tanya's youth grows duller.
Thus overcast with tempest gray
Sicklies the adolescent day.

IV. 24

Alas, Tatyana's bloom is blighted;
She droops and fades without a word,
Too numb at heart to be excited,
Her spirit utterly unstirred.
Sage heads are wagged and clucks are uttered,
Where neighbors gather, it is muttered:
She should be married with all speed!
But stay; I feel an urgent need
To vary this unwholesome ration
With taste of lovers' happiness;
I am constrained, I will confess,
My gentle readers, by compassion;
So bear with me and let it be:
My Tanya is so dear to me!

IV. 25

With each succeeding hour more sweetly
By Olga's youthful charms subdued,
Vladimir gave himself completely
To that delightful servitude.
They are as one; the morning hour
Finds them astroll in park or bower,
Arms linked, and in the evening gloom
They sit together in her room;
And then? Elated and affrighted
By love's shy urge, he would make bold
At most from time to time to hold—
By her indulgent smile invited—
A straying ringlet to caress,
Or kiss the border of her dress.

IV. 26

Or he would read her novels dwelling
On moral themes in earnest vein,
And by their nature lore excelling
Chateaubriand in his domain.
But as to certain worthless pages
(Half-baked and apt to prove outrageous
To maidens delicately bred)
He leaves them blushingly unread.
Sometimes at well-secluded station
They huddled, chin in hand, and pored
Over the chessmen on the board,
Sunk in profoundest contemplation,
Till Lensky with a musing look
With his own pawn struck his own rook.

IV. 27

At home, too, Olga's image never
Would fail to occupy him still;
Her album's airy leaves forever
Bear witness to his loving skill:
Here, delicately traced and tinted,
Pastoral vistas are imprinted,
A temple to the Lady Love,
A tombstone, or a lyre and dove;
There, on the pages of remembrance
Beneath the signing of a friend
A tender little verse is penned,
A pensive moment's muted semblance,
A fleeting daydream's feeble trace
That many years will not efface.

IV. 28

Those albums of a country maiden
You all have met with, I'll be bound:
Front, back, and sides scrawled up and laden
With sayings of perfervid sound.
There, all orthography defying,
Parade, unscanning but undying,
Those rhymes of faithful friendship's pledge,
Sprawled out or squeezed along an edge.
Atop page one you will find written
Qu'écrirez-vous sur ces tablettes?
Beneath it: *t. à v. Annette;*
And on the last page you are smitten
By "She who loves you more must sign
Her name and pledges under mine."

IV. 29

There you find any combination
Of torches, flowers, coupled hearts,
You read perfervent protestations
Of "tender love till death us part";
An epauletted poetaster
Elsewhere bequeathed some rhymed disaster;
In such an album, friends, I too
Am glad to write a line or two,
For there at least I am persuaded
That any old endearing phrase
Will earn me a benignant gaze,
And will not afterwards be graded
With knitted brow or chuckle snide
As to how expertly I lied.

IV. 30

But you, delinquent tomes astray from
The lending library of Hell,
That modish rhymesters shy away from,
Portentous albums, you repel;
You that are sedulously varnished
With Tolstoy's wondrous brush[1] and garnished
With Baratynsky's verses too,
May God's bolt smite and shrivel you!
When glittering hostesses come purring
With quarto tome and "would you care,"
I'm seized with panic and despair
And feel an epigram astir in
The dark recesses of my soul—
When all I'm asked is to pay toll!

IV. 31

No madrigals has Lensky written
For youthful Olga's album dear;
With artless love his stylus smitten,
He can't be cleverly austere.
Whatever ear or other senses
Discerned in her, his pen dispenses,
And like an elemental wave
His elegiacs foam and rave.
Thus you, Yazykov, bard enraptured,[2]
From some deep stirrings in your womb
Burst into song to God knows whom
And may imagine you have captured
In that rare elegiac freight
The sum and essence of your fate.

IV. 32

But hush! You hear? The critic quarrels,
Severely bids us lay aside
Our ragged elegiac laurels
And fretfully is heard to chide
Our guild of rhymers: "Quit your drivel,
Your everlasting changeless snivel
For once-there-was and used-to-be,
Sing us a new tune—change your key!"
You justly show us, sapient scoffer,
The trump, the dagger, and the mask,
From there and everywhere you ask
That we restock our empty coffer;
Not bravely spoken?—Wrong again!
"Odes you should write us, gentlemen."[3]

IV. 33

"Odes, as composed and instituted
Once in the mighty age of fame . . ."
So solemn odes alone are suited?
Come, friend, is it not all the same?
Does what the satirist indicted
And in "Their Views" so shrewdly cited[4]
Seem more congenial to you
Than what we mournful rhymers do?
"No sense in elegies, no moral,
Just disembodied, vain regret,
Whereas the ode's high goal is set
On the Exalted . . ." I could quarrel
With that, of course, but I foresee
'Twould bring two ages down on me.

IV. 34

As freedom's lover, glory's gallant,
His mind on stormy fancies fed,
Vladimir might have tried his talent
On odes—which Olga never read.
Your elegist, now, must be fearful
To face his love and read his tearful
Effusion to her! Yet than this,
They say, there is no higher bliss.
Yes—count the modest lover blessèd
Who may recite beneath the eyes
Of Her for whom he sings and sighs,
When she is languorously placid!
Though this, when all is said and done,
May not be her idea of fun.

IV. 35

My own harmonious contriving
I bring to my old Nanny's ears,
A crop of dreams for the surviving
Companion of my childhood years.
To chase a dull meal, I belabor
A stray and unsuspecting neighbor
By seizing hold of his lapel
And spouting blank verse by the ell,
Or else (and here the joke is over)
Beset by heartache and the Muse,
I wander by my lake and choose
To flush a flock of ducks from cover,
Who, hearing those sweet stanzas ring,
Break from the shoreline and take wing.

IV. 36[5]

And while I trace their distant travel,
A huntsman hidden in the trees
Will send all verses to the devil
And set his hammer back at ease.
By each his private game is plotted,
To each his own pursuit allotted:
One shoots at wild ducks in the sky;
One fools about with verse as I;
One slaps at flies with expert swatting;
One war for his amusement chose;
One cultivates exquisite woes;
One rules the crowd by clever plotting;
One finds his interest in wine,
And good and bad in all combine.

IV. 37

Well, and Onegin? Brothers, patience!
Don't hurry on this tale of mine:
In time his daily occupations
Will be reported here in fine.
Eugene lived in a hermit's heaven:
In summer he arose at seven
And lightly sauntered to a rill
That washed the bottom of his hill;
In tribute to Gülnare's singer[6]
He swam his Hellespontus too,
Then drank his coffee, leafing through
Some journal with disdainful finger
And dressed . . .

(IV. 38)

IV. 39

Reposeful slumber, reading, rambling,
The purl of brooks, the sylvan shades,
Betweentimes fresh young kisses sampling
From creamy-skinned and black-eyed maids,
An eager mount, to rein obedient,
Light dinner taken when expedient,
A glass or two of gleaming wine,
Seclusion, hush: thus in divine
Simplicity his life proceeded;
Unfeelingly, without a care,
He sipped its sweetness, unaware
Of summer's shining gait; unheeded
Alike his urban friends and treats
And tedious holiday conceits.

IV. 40

But then, our northern summer season
Like southern winter comes, and lo,
Is gone; and though for some odd reason
We won't admit it, it is so.
Autumn was in the air already,
The sun's gay sparkle grew unsteady,
The timeless day became more brief;
The forest, long in darkling leaf,
Unclothed itself with mournful rustle;
The fields were wrapped in misty fleece,
A raucous caravan of geese
Winged southward; after summer's bustle
A duller season was at hand:
November hovered overland.

IV. 41

Through frigid haze the dawn resurges,
Abroad the harvest sounds abate;
And soon the hungry wolf emerges
Upon the highway with his mate.
The scent scares into snorting flurries
The trudging horse; the traveler hurries
His way uphill in wary haste.
No longer are the cattle chased
Out of the byre at dawn, the thinning
Horn-notes of cowherds cease the tune
That rounds them up again at noon.
Indoors the maiden sings at spinning
Before the crackling pine-flare light,
Companion of the winter night.

IV. 42

At last a crackling frost enfolded
Fields silvered o'er with early snows:
(All right—who am I to withold it,
The rhyme you knew was coming—ROSE)[7]
The ice-clad river's polished luster
No stylish ballroom floor could muster;
A joyous swarm of urchins grates
The frozen sheet with ringing skates.
A cumbrous goose on ruddy paddies
Comes waddling down the bank to swim,
Steps gingerly across the rim,
Slithers and falls; in swirling eddies
Descends the virgin snow and pranks
And showers stars upon the banks.

IV. 43

What in those winter-bound recesses
To do? Take walks? One must agree,
The somber countryside depresses
With its austere monotony.
Across the frozen steppes to gallop?
Your horse, its iron's blunted scallop
Caught on a vicious icy clot,
Will have a fall, as like as not.
Stay in your cell and read: the highlights
Are Pradt[8] and Walter Scott. No good?
Not interested? Well, you could
Check ledgers, sulk, drink—the long twilights
Will somehow pass, tomorrow's too,
And so the whole gay winter through!

IV. 44

Childe Harold-like, Eugene subsided
Into a state of pensive sloth:
Straight from the drowsy bed he glided
Into his tub through icy froth,
Then spent all day at home with balking
Account books, or from morning stalking
The table, playing solo pool,
A blunt old cue his only tool.
The cue is shelved, billiards forgotten
At evenfall; Onegin waits,
While by the fire they lay the plates:
At last here comes a troika trotting,
Turns in; they're Lensky's iron-grays;
To table now, and no two ways!

IV. 45

Without delay the host produces—
Well-frosted on the table set—
The blissful and benignant juices
Of Veuve Cliquot or of Moët.
They spark with Hippocrene's twinkle,
Their effervescent froth and tinkle
(Symbolical of what you will)
Once held me captive; do you still
Recall, friends, how I would surrender
My last coin for them long ago?
Ah, yes, their wonder-working flow,
What foolish froth did it engender,
How many jokes, poetic dreams,
What quarrels, what delightful schemes!

IV. 46

But now my stomach starts demurring
From such ebullient fizz, and so
These days I find myself preferring
The bland and sensible Bordeaux.
Nor have I left enough resilience
For Aÿ,[9] with its verve and brilliance
Of a young mistress, moody, vain,
Contrary-headed, and inane . . .
But you, Bordeaux, are like a steady
Lifetime companion who in care
Stands by us here and everywhere
To render service, ever ready
Soothing tranquillity to lend.
Long live Bordeaux, our faithful friend!

IV. 47

The fire grew fainter, scarcely seething,
The golden embers sank in dust,
Barely perceptible, the wreathing
Smoke-wisps ascend, the chimney just
A breath of warmth. The pipe-smoke dwindled
Into the flue, the wine-flask kindled
A gleam where yet it stood and hissed.
The window dimmed with evening mist.
I like a friendly chat in season,
I like to share a friendly glass
About the hour that people class
As "wolf-and-dog time" (for some reason
That I for one could never see).
Here's our companions' colloquy:

IV. 48

"How are your friends, let me inquire,
Tatyana, and your own dear belle?"
"Here, fill my glass a little higher—
Enough, my dear. They are all well,
And all have asked to be commended
To you. Oh, my dear friend, how splendid
Have Olga's shoulders grown, her bust!
Ah, and her soul! . . . Some time we must
Look in again; you surely owe them
The favor; really, was it nice
To show your face there once or twice
Then act as though you did not know them?
Oh . . . I'm a dunce, I do declare!
This Saturday you will be there!"

IV. 49

"I?" "Yes, Olinka and her mother
Have asked me to invite you too;
It's Tanya's name-day—surely, brother,
It is the least that you can do!"
"There'll be a frightful crowd and babble,
A crush of every kind of rabble . . ."
"Oh, nonsense, not like that at all!
Who should be there? Just kin, that's all.
Let's go, you too, just as a favor!
What do you say?" "All right." "How nice!"
With this he emptied in a trice
His glass, a toast to his dear neighbor,
And then he spread himself once more
About his Olga. Love's a bore!

IV. 50

Lensky was gay. Fulfillment's hour
Was set a fortnight after this,
And love's intoxicating flower,
The mysteries of wedded bliss
Held out their lure in life's tomorrow.
Hymen's contrariness and sorrow,
His dank eternity of yawns
Upon this dreamer never dawns.
While we, his critics, cannot mention
Homelife but as appalling rows
Of sentimentalists' tableaus
Worthy of Lafontaine's[10] invention,
Poor Lensky was by mind and heart
Cut out for the domestic part.

IV. 51

He was beloved . . . or, to amend it,
He thought he was, and thought it bliss.
Blest they who can, their doubts suspended,
All frigid reasoning dismiss,
And find an ease as all-consoling
As roadside drunks on inn-beds lolling,
Or, gentler, butterflies that cling
To honeyed blossoms in the spring.
But wretched, whose foreboding vision,
Whose wakeful mind is never blurred,
To whom each movement, every word
Spells shame and breeds a cold derision;
Whose heart experience has cooled
And bars from being sweetly fooled!

1825–26.

Notes

1. F. P. Tolstoy, an erudite contemporary painter and medallionist, whose prestige helped to make the non-literary arts respectable among the Russian aristocracy.

2. N. M. Yazykov (1803–46), a minor poet, Pushkin's close contemporary, friend, and former boon companion.

3. "A retort by Pushkin (see *Works,* ed. Morozov, III.315 note) to his friend Küchelbecker, who had urged in the journal *Mnemosyne* that 'elegies', and Pushkin's in particular, were a species inferior to the ode, which contained more 'rapture' (*vostorg*) and more poetry. In a prose note of 1824 (*id.,* V. 21) Pushkin returns to the charge, saying that the ode is the lowest kind of poem, being destitute of 'plan', and that mere 'rapture' excludes the kind of 'tranquillity' (*spokoystviye*) which is 'an indispensable condition of the highest beauty'—a remark reminding one of a famous phrase by his contemporary, Wordsworth. 'Elegy', in the above stanzas, means any short meditative lyric, not necessarily melancholy" (Professor O. Elton's note). "The trump, the dagger, and the mask"—emblems of the classical drama.

4. I. I. Dmitriev (1760–1837), chief exponent and practitioner of the light, elegant style in poetry that arose toward the end of the eighteenth century in reaction against the high-flown classicists, had written *Chuzhoy Tolk,* a satire on writers of odes.

5. This stanza was omitted after the first edition of 1826.

6. Byron, in *The Corsair.*

7. Dmitry Čiževsky in the commentary to his edition of *Eugene Onegin* (Harvard University Press, Cambridge, 1953, p. 253) remarks that "this passage is a protest, put in humorous form, against the poverty and traditional character of Russian rhymes; incidentally it serves to remind the reader of the 'light' tone of the novel. These complaints about Russian rhymes have continued up to the present . . ." However, unlike Vyazemsky and later poets, Pushkin evidently did not think this poverty a flaw inherent in the Russian lexicon, but rather a failing on the part of its users. The ubiquity and versatility of function of the standard suffixes of Russian nominal and verbal flexion actually open up a vast reservoir of rhymes, both masculine and feminine. The great majority of Pushkin's rhymes are of this kind. By contrast, practically all English masculine rhymes (there being few end-stressed suffixes like the French-derived -ee) must rely on root words, thus presenting a far more stringent metrical problem.

8. Dominique de Pradt (1759–1837), French archbishop and diplomat, prominent from the *ancien régime* to the restoration period; a prolific and popular political essayist.

9. Aÿ, a champagne from the Marne region. In his note to this passage, Pushkin quotes some lines from *Message to L.P.* in which "poetic Aÿ" with its whispering foam is associated with heedless youth and love.

10. The German Huguenot, August Lafontaine, military chaplain and tireless writer of sentimental novels.

Chapter
Five

Know not those fearsome dreams,

O my Svetlana!

ZHUKOVSKY

V. 1

Fall lingered on as if it never
Would leave the countryside that year,
While Nature seemed to wait forever
For winter. Snow did not appear
Till the third January morning.
Up early, Tanya without warning
Finds roofs and fences overnight
Turned to exhilarating white,
Her window laced with subtle etching,
The trees with wintry silver starrred,
Pert magpies sporting in the yard,
The softly covered hilltops stretching
'Neath winter's scintillating pall . . .
And clear is all, and white is all.

V. 2

Winter . . . the peasant, feeling festive,
Breaks a new trail with sledge and horse;
Sensing the snow, his nag is restive
And manages a trot of sorts;
Here passes, powdery furrows tracing,
A spirited kibítka, racing,
The coachman on his box a flash
Of sheepskin coat and crimson sash.
There runs a yard-boy, having chosen
To seat his "Rover" on the sled,
Himself hitched up in horse's stead;
The rascal rubs one finger, frozen
Already, with a wince and grin,
While Mother shakes her fist within.

V. 3

To you this kind of nature writing
May be of limited allure;
It's all low-style and unexciting,
Shows scant refinement, to be sure.
A bard of more exuberant lyre,[1]
With inspiration's god afire,
Portrayed the virgin snow for you
And winter's charms in every hue:
I dare say you're devoted to him
As he depicts with lyric glow
Clandestine outings in the snow;
I've no intention to outdo him
Or challenge him in this regard,
Nor you, the Finland maiden's bard![2]

V. 4

To Tanya (Russian in her feeling,
Though unaware why this should be),
The Russian winter was appealing
In all its frigid majesty;
On sunny days, the hoarfrost's sparkle,
The sleighs, and when the heavens darkle,
The snows aglow with rosy lights,
The misty January nights.
The Twelfth-night's immemorial tenor
Held sway amongst them as of old:
Young ladies had their fortunes told
By kerchiefed sibyls of the manor,
Who every year presaged once more
Husbands in uniform, and war.

V. 5

Tatyana, credulously dwelling
In simple folkways of the past,
Believed in dreams and fortune-telling
And heeded what the moon forecast.
Portents and omens would distress her,
And random incidents impress her
With some occult significance
Or dire foreboding of mischance.
A preening pussycat, relaxing
Upon the stove with lick and purr,
Was an unfailing sign to her
That guests were coming; or a waxing
Twin-horned young moon that she saw **ride**
Across the sky on her left side

V. 6

Would make her tremble and change **color;**
Each time a shooting star might flash
In the dark firmament, grow duller
And burst asunder into ash:
All flustered, Tanya would be seeking,
While yet the fiery spark was streaking,
To whisper it her heart's desire.
But if she met a black-robed friar
At any place or any season,
Or if from out the meadow swath
A fleeing hare should cross her path,
She would be frightened out of reason,
And filled with superstitious dread,
See some calamity ahead.

V. 7

Why not? Those very same afflictions
Afforded her a secret glee,
Which Nature, fond of contradictions,
Has planted deep in you and me.
The feast is here; what joy amongst us!
The fates are probed by flighty youngsters
Who feel that anything's worth while,
Whom life's infinities beguile,
All luminous beyond conceiving,
And by bespectacled old age
Who, bowing out on darkened stage,
Have lost it all beyond retrieving;
What matter: hope's deceptive wisp
Belies it with its childish lisp.

V. 8

Tatyana curiously gazes
At the prophetic waxen mold,
All eager in its wondrous mazes
A wondrous future to behold.
Then from the basin someone dredges,
Ring after ring, the players' pledges,
And comes her ringlet, they rehearse
The immemorial little verse:
"There all the serfs are wealthy yeomen,
They shovel silver with a spade;
To whom we sing, he shall be made
Famous and rich!" But for ill omen
They take this plaintive ditty's voice;
Koshurka is the maidens' choice.[3]

V. 9

The night is frosty, bright all heaven,
The lofty lanterns' wondrous choir
Wheels on, serenely calm and even . . .
Tatyana steps in loose attire
Out on the spacious courtyard, training
Her mirror at the moon;[4] but waning
In the dark glass, there wanly shone
The melancholy moon alone . . .
Hark . . . footsteps crunch the snow; tiptoeing
Up to the passerby she bounds,
Hails him; the girlish treble sounds
More tuneful than the reed pipe's blowing:
"What is your name?" He stares, and on
He strides, replying: "Agafon."[5]

V. 10

Tatyana, by her nanny bidden,
Prepared to call on spirit sight,
And in the bathhouse ordered, hidden
From all, two beds laid out that night.
But sudden dread befell Tatyana . . .
And I, too—thinking of Svetlana,[6]
A dread befell me—never mind . . .
We will not be with her, I find,
To conjure. Now Tatyana, shedding
Her sash, undressed and went to bed,
Lel on the wing above her head,[7]
Beneath it, in the downy bedding
The girlish mirror nestled deep.
All's hushed. Tatyana is asleep.

V. 11

And dreams a dream of wondrous strangeness.
She seems to walk a wintry field,
A clearing set in snowy ranges,
By dreary vapors half concealed.
Ahead, between the snowdrifts rushing
Its angry waters, swirling, gushing,
In somber grayness roars and strains
A stream, still free of winter's chains.
Two boughs which ice has fused together
Here form a parlous swaying plank
To join the near and further bank;
Distraught, uncertain where and whether
To dare the roaring torrent's wrath,
Tatyana halted in her path.

V. 12

The stream, like rankling separation,
Moves her to chide it, as it were;
There's no one at the further station
To stretch a helping hand to her;
But there—a snowdrift heaves and surges,
And from beneath it who emerges?
A bear, disheveled all and swarth;
Tanya cries out, he stretches forth
A mighty paw with razor talons
And growls; she with a shrinking hand
Supports herself upon it, and
In tremulously halting balance
Is borne across the torrent there;
And then—the bear comes after her!

V. 13

She dares no backward glance, unable
To spur her hurried steps enough,
And still the groom in shaggy sable
Refuses to be shaken off;
Still onward crashed the fiend and shuffled.
Woods loom ahead; tall pines unruffled
In their beclouded beauty frown,
Their sloping branches all weighed down
With pads of snow. Through the denuded
Treetops of linden, birch, and ash
The rays of heaven's lanterns flash.
No path leads here; all blurred and hooded
The brush and hillsides rise and fall,
Enveloped deep in snowy pall.

V. 14

She gains the wood, the bear in rushing
Pursuit, knee-high in fluffy snow,
Long branches claw at her, now brushing
About her throat, now from below
Her golden earrings roughly ripping,
Then through the trackless snowdrifts tripping,
A sodden sandal's wrenched away;
Her kerchief's next to go astray;
But she is loath to turn or linger,
Lest in the rear the bear should press
Too close; ashamed in her distress
To lift her hem with shaking finger,
She flounders on, he on her trail,
Until her strength begins to fail.

V. 15

She sinks into the snow; her massive
Pursuer lifts her up with zeal,
While she, insensible and passive,
Has ceased to breathe or stir or feel.
Along a forest trail she's carried:
There lurks a lowly hovel, buried
In trees, half sunken out of sight
In mounds of desert snow. A light
Is winking brightly from a dormer,
The hut resounds with roars and yells:
The bear spoke: Here my gossip dwells,
Sit by his side, and you'll be warmer!
And on the threshold she was dropped
While he went in and never stopped.

V. 16

Tatyana looks, her faintness passes,
She's in the hall still, gone the bear;
Next door they hoot and clink their glasses,
As if a wake were held in there;
Here nothing human meets her glances,
And so she stealthily advances,
Peeps through the crack—what does she see!
There sits a monstrous company
At table: antlered, greyhound-snouted
Was one; a witch, goat-whiskered freak,
Another; next with comb and beak
A cock's head; there proud Jack-Bones pouted;
A bobtailed dwarf beyond him sat,
And here a thing half crane, half cat.

V. 17

More freaks, more horrors are discovered:
A prawn and spider pickaback,
A skull in scarlet nightcap hovered
Atop a goose's swivel-neck,
A windmill kicked its heels a-dancing,
Its whirling flippers thrashing, prancing,
Guffaw, bark, whistle, hoot, and flop,
Mixed human clamor, horses' clop.
How she was stunned, although, in that hovel
To see amidst the loathly stir
The one both dear and dread to her,
The hero of the present novel!
Onegin too was seated there,
And gave the door a furtive stare.

V. 18

He makes a sign—the others scurry;
He drinks—they duly roar and swill;
He laughs—all cackle in a hurry,
He frowns—and everyone is still.
He clearly ruled here. Interested
More than aghast now, Tanya rested
A cautious hand against the door
And opened it a little more . . .
A sudden gust blows up, more dimly
Now flicker the nocturnal lights;
Confusion strikes the band of sprites;
His eyes agleam, Onegin grimly
Stands up with thunder on the floor;
All rise. He strides toward the door.

V. 19

Tatyana quakes, in desperation
She strains to run as though from death:
Quite useless; writhing in frustration,
She tries to scream, but not a breath
Will issue. Now Eugene advances,
Thrusts wide the door, and to the glances
Of Hell's own spooks she stands revealed;
Their raucous laughter shrilled and squealed;
All eyes on her; proboscis twisted,
Hoof, whisker, bushy-crested tail,
Horn, blood-red tongue, all lash and flail,
And arms unfleshed and bony-fisted
All point and rampantly entwine
With one great roar: She's mine! She's mine!

V. 20

She's mine! Eugene pronounces grimly,
The gang dissolves at his dread tone;
In chilly murk she senses dimly
Eugene and she are left alone.
He gently has half-led, half-borne her
To a rough trestle in the corner
And eased her onto this frail bed
And to her shoulder bent his head . . .
When of a sudden Olga enters,
Lensky behind her; lanterns shine;
Onegin makes an angry sign
And glares about him, brows portentous,
And chides the uninvited pair;
Tatyana lies half senseless there.

V. 21

Their angry voices swell; a dagger's
Long blade glints in his hand, he springs,
And in an instant Lensky staggers
And falls; more dense the gloom; out rings
A desolate shriek . . . the hovel quivers,
And terror-struck, Tatyana shivers
And wakes . . . Already daylight reigns,
Her window through its frosted panes
Filters the ruby dawn. In rushes
Olga, her footfall swallow-light,
Her color up more rosy-bright
Than northerly Aurora's blushes;
"Now you must tell me all," says she,
"What did you dream? Whom did you see?"

V. 22

But unaware of Olga's bustle,
She hugs a book in bed with her,
Her fingers fly, the pages rustle,
She's too engrossed to speak or hear.
This book between its boards encases
No honey-sweet poetic graces,
No pretty prints, no insights keen,
Yet neither Vergil nor Racine,
Nor Seneca's, Scott's, Byron's pages,
Nor even fashion plates can boast
Addicts so utterly engrossed:
The high priest of Chaldean sages,
Martin Zadeka, it was he,
The dreamer's oracle and key.[8]

V. 23

This fountain of unfathomed learning
Had come to her secluded nook
When a stray peddler was sojourning
Nearby; from him she bought the book.
She had to throw into the barter,
Besides three rubles and a quarter,
Malvine,[9] Part Two, then had to add
Two grammars and a Petriad,[10]
A fable-book of vulgar diction,
And Marmontel (just Volume Three).
Martin Zadeka came to be
Tanya's chief treasure; in affliction
None surer solace can confer,
And every night he sleeps with her.

V. 24

By her nocturnal visions frightened,
Uncertain what those horrors meant,
Tatyana seeks to be enlightened
What clues to their occult intent
The subject index might afford her;
She finds in alphabetic order
The entries: Bear, Bench, Blizzard, Briar,
Bridge, Dagger, Darkness, Feasting, Fire,
And so on. But for once the Master
Has no reply to what she asks,
The dream still ominously masks
Tidings of sadness and disaster.
For days to follow she will find
Its riddles preying on her mind.

V. 25

The day by Eos' rosy fingers
From vales of morn is ushered clear,
And close behind the sun[11] there lingers
The name-day with its festive cheer.
Since dawn the guests have started filling
The manor, clans of neighbors spilling
Full-muster from calash and chaise,
Kibitkas, britskas, landaus, sleighs.
They mill and bustle on the landing,
New entries meet with well-bred fuss,
Lap dogs are yapping, flappers buss,
Guffaw and hubbub, crowds expanding
With bow and scrape and clicking heel,
While nannies scold and babies squeal.

V. 26

Here Pustyakóv comes with his consort,
Both amply built, with chubby cheeks,
And there Gvozdín, who wisely sponsored
Fat farms and destitute muzhiks;
The silver-haired Skotínins sported
Offspring of every age, assorted
From thirty down to two or so;
Here's Petyushkóv, the district beau,
My own first cousin, too, Buyánov,[12]
In vizored cap and downy fluff
(As you no doubt remember him);
Plump Councilor (retd.) Flyánov,
Who savored gossip, bribes, and jokes;
A glutton, rogue, and walking hoax.

V. 27

The Kharlikóvs have brought their lodger,
Monsieur Triquet, in their own rig,
Late from Tambóv, a sly old codger
In spectacles and ginger wig.
True Gaul, he carried in his purselet
For Tanya's day a festive verselet,
Set to the childhood melody:
Réveillez-vous, belle endormie.
This, found among old songs inserted
In some bemildewed almanac,
He had—the poet must not lack
Invention—rescued and converted,
With bold resource for *belle Nina*
Supplying *belle Tatyana.*

V. 28

And here, from his adjacent station,
The solace of provincial moms,
All nubile maidens' inspiration,
The Company Commander comes.
He brings—what news, what priceless tiding:
The regimental band comes riding
To play here, by the Colonel's call.
Oh, ecstasy: there'll be a ball!
The girls already skip with rapture;
But dinner first. The married pairs
Take in each other, beaus seeks chairs
Across from Tanya, girls to capture
Seats close to her; the buzzing troop
All cross themselves before the soup.

V. 29

Now for a time subsides the chatter;
All mouths are full, on every side
The silver clinks, the dishes clatter,
And glasses ringingly collide.
At length with each succeeding potion
More guests join in the grand commotion;
Nobody listens; cross-talk, peals
Of laughter, arguments, and squeals.
A door flies open: Lensky! Lagging
Behind, Onegin, too. "Oh, dear!"
The hostess cries. "At last you're here!"
The guests move over; with much dragging
Of chairs and plates and much to-do
They make some room and seat the two.

V. 30

They face Tatyana without warning
Across the table, and she pales
More wanly than the moon at morning,
Nor hind more tremulously quails
At bay; her shadowed eyes unwilling
To rise, fierce blaze within her thrilling
And stifling her, she does not hear
The friends' salutes, her eyes are near
To brimming over; yet, half ready
To faint, poor girl, from sheer dismay,
She makes good sense resume its sway;
Scarce audible, her lips unsteady,
She lisps some phrase with fair good grace
And bravely settles in her place.

V. 31

Girls' tragico-hysteric vapors,
Their swoons and tears had long unmanned
Eugene, who felt that of such capers
He'd sampled all that he could stand.
Galled as he was to waspish anger
By this gross feast, the maiden's languor,
Her tremors, did not soothe his spite;
Unwilling to endure the sight,
He looked the other way; indignant
At Lensky's treachery, he swore
To drive him wild and pay the score.
Meanwhile in premature malignant
Enjoyment he begins to trace
Mental cartoons of every face.

V. 32

Tatyana's plight, of course, was noted
Not by Eugene alone; but now
Their scrutiny was all devoted
To a plump pie that made its bow
(But proved too salt, alas!). Already
In pitch-sealed flasks arrives the heady
Champagne 'twixt meat-course and blancmange,
And in its wake, in serried range,
The glass that slimly, trimly tapers,
So like your slender waist, Zizi,
Heart's crystal, you that used to be
Game for my first poetic capers,
Allurement's phial that I adored,
Drunk with the wine of love you poured!

V. 33

The cork was loosened, and in flaring
Upsurge of foam the wine was freed,
Lisped in the glass; with stately bearing,
Long tantalized by his own screed,
Triquet arose at last; abated
All chatter, the assembly waited.
Tatyana shrank; he took his stand
And turning to her, script in hand,
Gave voice, off-key. They cheered, applauded,
And forced Tatyana for reward
To drop a curtsy to the bard;
But he, demure, though highly lauded,
Is first to toast her, *sans hauteur*,
And hands the madrigal to her.

V. 34

Now came good wishes, commendations;
Tatyana answered by the book.
But when Eugene's congratulations
Were due in turn, the girl's wan look,
Embarrassment, exhausted languor,
Moved him to sympathy, not anger;
And while he made a silent bow,
A glance went with it which, somehow,
Was strangely tender. Was it really
The touch of pity at his heart,
Or did he act the amorous part
From kindness, or by habit merely?
But tenderness it did express,
And Tanya warmed to its caress.

V. 35

Their chairs pushed back with noisy scraping,
The guests into the parlor squeeze,
As from the murmurous hive escaping
To tempting crops, a swarm of bees.
Complacent after festive browsing
Now neighbor faces neighbor drowsing,
The matrons round the fire group,
Elsewhere the girls in whispering troop.
Soon green-baize tables have invaded
The scene; while l'Ombre and Boston win
The older addicts, Whist is "in";
And still its glamour has not faded:
A gamy breed, all equal-born,
All avid boredom's worthless spawn.

V. 36

Eight rubbers have the kings and aces
Of whist played off in one long spell,
Eight times they have exchanged their places;
Now tea is brought. I like to tell
The hours' advancing, like the locals.
By luncheon, dinner, tea; we yokels
Keep track of time without much fuss;
Our stomachs watch the clock for us.
I notice here a certain penchant
To let my stanzas overflow
With food and drink (this apropos);
As many feasts and sprees are mentioned
As you, great Homeros, devised,
Whom thirty ages idolized!

(V. 37, 38)

V. 39

But tea is served. With dainty breeding
The girls have hardly touched the cup,
When from the hall next door proceeding,
The sound of horn and flute wells up.
His glass of tea with rum abandoned,
Petyushkov thrills to the command, and,
Fair Paris of provincial balls,
Engages Olga. Lensky calls
Upon Tatyana. Kharlikova,
A damsel ripe in years, is off
With our sly poet from Tambóv.
Buyánov snatches Pustyakóva,
And all debouch into the hall,
Where in its splendor shines the ball.

V. 40

I started, early in my story,
To conjure up (see Chapter One)
St. Petersburg in ballroom glory,
As old Albani[13] might have done;
But then, by idle dreams deflected,
With reminiscences infected,
I sang of feet I knew before . . .
Dear girlish feet, it's time no more
On your slim trail to court distraction:
Time, at the turning of my youth,
To prove that I am less uncouth,
And, come of age in craft and action,
Can keep this Chapter Five as free
Of such digressions as may be.

V. 41

As unreflecting and unfading
As life's young pulse that never halts,
Pair after wheeling pair parading,
Revolved the pulsing, stirring waltz.
Now the revenge that he was after
Is near: Eugene, with inward laughter,
Steps up to Olga and requests
The waltz; in view of all the guests
They sway and whirl; next, having seated
His lady, he displays his charm
In small-talk, then extends his arm,
And the performance is repeated.
The ballroom buzzes with surprise,
And Lensky can't believe his eyes.

V. 42

Now the Mazurka . . . Where it pounded
Its thunderous beat in former days,
The ballroom end to end resounded
As stamping heels shook the parquets
And set the startled windows ringing;
Now, lady-like, demurely swinging,
On lacquered boards we slide and curve,
And only country towns preserve
The pristine glories duly polished:
High heels, moustachios, saltos bold
Grace the Mazurka as of old
Where they have never been abolished
By Fashion's tyranny, the prime
Disease of Russia in our time.

(V. 43)

V. 44

My boisterous cousin, moving deftly
To where he sees Onegin stand,
Brings Olga and Tatyana. Swiftly
Onegin chooses Olga's hand.
He leads her, nonchalantly gliding,
And whispers in her ear, confiding
Some compliment with tender pose,
Presses her hand . . . The color rose
To her vain cheek a little higher
At this. Vladimir's eyes devoured
The little scene: he flushed and glowered
With jealous outrage all on fire,
Saw the Mazurka over, and
For the cotillion asked her hand.

V. 45

But no, she can't. Can't? Strange behavior!
No, she's already pledged this dance
To Eugene. What? O Lord and Savior!
Not this! Could she, by any chance . . .
It can't be . . . Olga, scarce unswaddled,
Become a flirt, a flighty coddled
Coquette, adroit to trick and vex,
Old in the falsehood of her sex?
This stunning blow is past his bearing;
Cursing all women who betray,
He's out, and mounted, and away.
Now let a brace of pistols flaring,
A pair of bullets, nothing more,
Decide his fate and square the score.

1826.

Notes

1. "See *First Snow,* a poem by Prince Vyazemsky" (Pushkin's note).

2. "See the description of a Finnish winter in the *Edda* by Baratynsky" (Pushkin's note).

3. " 'The tom calls his pussy/ To the stove-niche to sleep'; prophecy of a wedding, while the first ditty presages death" (Pushkin's note). *Koshurka* is the pussycat. Rites like this rings-in-a-dish fortune-telling with ancient rhymes are still practiced on St. Sylvester's day (New Year's Eve) in parts of Europe, especially pouring molten lead into a dish of water and casting fortunes from the fantastic shapes that emerge. The first part of the stanza evidently alludes to wax-casting for the same purpose.

4. "In this way one finds out the name of one's bridegroom-to-be" (Pushkin's note).

5. Many of these Greek calendar names, like the rustic American Rube or Lem, have distinctly bucolic connotations. Agafon here provides a comic anticlimax to Tatyana's romantic quest.

6. Svetlana, eponymous heroine of Zhukovsky's melodramatic ballad of the supernatural (1812), a partial imitation of Bürger's famous *Lenore.*

7. Lel, according to a dubious tradition, was the Old Slavic divinity corresponding to the Greek Hymen.

8. "Dream-books are published with us under the imprint of Martin Zadeka, a respectable man who never wrote any, as B. M. Fyodorov points out" (Pushkin's note).

9. Title of a novel by Mme. Cottin, author of the popular romance of Malek-Adhel (also Note 3, page 85).

10. A "Petriad" was a heroic poem about Peter the Great, several of which had wide currency at the time.

11. Here Pushkin parodies some well-known lines from a poem by Lomonosov, which he quotes in a note.

12. A playful allusion to one Buyanov who figures with these attributes in a poem by Pushkin's uncle, V. L. Pushkin Buyanov, being a child of his uncle's intellect, thus becomes Pushkin's "cousin."

13. Francesco Albani, Italian baroque painter.

Chapter Six

La sotto i giorni nubilosi e brevi

Nasce una gente a cui l'morir non dole.

PETRARCH

VI. 1

Aware that Vladimir had vanished,
Eugene, again by boredom teased,
Sulked—all concern with Olga banished,
Now his resentment was appeased.
And his distraction proves contagious;
Her eyes seek Lensky's face; for ages
The long cotillion's figures seem
To drag like an oppressive dream.
At last it ends. They go to supper.
In every nook where sleepers might
Be bedded down to spend the night
Sheets blossom forth, from hall to upper
Maids' quarters. All need rest. Eugene,
Sole home-bound guest, departs the scene.

VI. 2

And peace reigns; from the parlor hisses
The snore of portly Pustyakóv,
Commingled with his portly Missus'.
Gvozdín, Buyánov, Petyushkóv,
And Flyánov, slightly heavy-headed,
On banked-up dining chairs were bedded,
While on the floor Monsieur Triquet
In flannel waist and nightcap lay.
The maidens quartered with Tatyana
And Olga lay in slumber deep.
Alone poor Tanya did not sleep,
But in the radiance of Diana
Sat sadly by the window and
Gazed out across the somber land.

VI. 3

His call today, so unexpected,
The fleeting fondness in his eyes,
The strange maneuver he enacted
With Olga, sorely exercise
Her doubting soul; in vain she wonders
What it might mean, and bleakly ponders,
By darts of jealous anguish stung,
As if an icy hand had wrung
Her heart, or fathomless and fearful,
Black deeps beneath her yawned and spun . . .
She murmurs: "I shall be undone;
Undone by him, I will be cheerful,
Nor rail at Fate's decree. Why live?
He has no happiness to give."

VI. 4

Onward, my story, faster, faster!
Here's a new face to be beheld:
Five versts from Lensky, who was master
At Krasnogorye manor, dwelled
In philosophic isolation
(And thrives today at his old station)
Zaretsky, once a rowdy sheik,
Commander of the card-fiends' clique,
Roué-in-chief and tavern-plyer,
But now all kindness and well-bred,
A good papá, although unwed,
A faithful friend, a peaceful squire,
And even, lo, an honest man:
Such progress in a life's brief span!

VI. 5

Time was when worldly toadies keenly
Extolled his evil feats of strength:
And true, his pistol punctured cleanly
An ace at seven fathoms' length;
True, too, that once, in splendid fettle,
In combat he had proved his mettle
By boldly plunging in the mud
From off his steed of Kalmyk stud,
Drunk as a king, and suffered capture
By French patrols: a priceless catch!
Just Regulus has met his match:
He would resume those bonds with rapture
To seek Very's [1] each day and drain
(On tick) three bottles there again.

VI. 6

He was amusing when he twitted,
Or led some blockhead off the track,
Or even fooled the quicker-witted
Overtly or behind his back;
And while some pranks he perpetrated
Were painfully reciprocated,
And though he found himself not once
Caught in a pitfall like a dunce,
He shone in cheerful disputation
With blunt or pointed repartee,
At proper times would silent be
Or gabble, both with calculation;
When hotheads glared, he stoked their spite
Till both were spoiling for a fight,

VI. 7

Or brought reluctant foes together
To share the love-feast as their guest,
Then blacked their names to others, whether
In slander or in harmless jest.
Sed alia tempora! Effusion
Of spirits, like its twin delusion,
Love's dream, with youth has ever fled;
And my Zaretsky, as I said,
—Pea-trees in fluffy bloom becalming
This refuge from a stormier age—
Lives like a veritable sage,
Plants cabbages like Horace farming,
Tends geese and ducks, and at his knee
The children learn their ABC.

VI. 8

He was no fool, and while his merit
Was not his heart, Onegin found
He savored his judicious spirit
And thought him sensible and sound.
Thus, having spent odd hours of leisure
In his good company with pleasure,
Eugene was not surprised at all
To see him pay an early call.
Zaretsky, salutations ended,
Before the chat could well begin,
Abruptly gave him with a grin
A note from Lensky's hand, intended
For him. He turned aside and read
In private what the poet said.

VI. 9

It was a challenge to a duel,
Urbane, high-minded, and polite;
In language cool, concise, and cruel,
He called Onegin out to fight.
Onegin, after quick perusal,
Too quick to think of a refusal,
Turned to the envoy who had brought
This kind of message with a taut
"At your command." Zaretsky hastened
To rise, "afraid he couldn't stay,
Much work at home," and drove away.
But left alone, Onegin, chastened,
Reviewed his conduct with some shame
And could not free himself of blame.

VI. 10

And rightly so: for self-indicted
In secret court, he could defend
But little, and was sternly cited
For many wrongs: First, that a friend,
Who loved so tenderly and gently,
Last night was duped so nonchalantly.
And second: if that friend had been
A silly ass, well, at eighteen
He could be pardoned. Not to mention
That he, who dearly loved the youth,
Ought to have proved himself in truth
No helpless play-ball of convention,
No gamecock bristling with offense,
But man of honor and good sense.

VI. 11

He could have curbed his angry feeling,
Instead of snarling; have appeased
That hot young spirit by appealing
To reason, friendship—had he pleased.
"But it's too late; that chance was squandered . . .
And now, to make things worse," he pondered,
"We're saddled with this dueling hawk,
Sharp, fond of gossip, quick to talk . . .
The best, of course, is to ignore him;
But still, one will not be exempt
From snickers, whispers, fools' contempt . . ."
Our god, Good Repute, rose before him,
To which we feel our honor bound:
This is what makes the world go round!

VI. 12

Lensky, with restless fury seething,
Awaits the answer to his writ,
And here his chatty neighbor, breathing
Solemnity, returns with it.
Oh, how the jealous heart exulted!
The constant fear of the insulted
Was that the rogue might with some jest
Extract himself and turn his breast
Away from where the pistol pointed.
Now all uncertainty is still:
Tomorrow morning by the mill,
Before the dawn they were appointed,
To cock their hammers eye to eye
And aim at temple or at thigh.

VI. 13

Determined to despise the cruel
Coquette, Vladimir meant to shun
All truck with her before the duel,
Kept looking at the clock, the sun . . .
And promptly, shrugging off the notion,
Flew to her door. That mixed emotion
He thought that Olga would betray
On seeing him, that pained dismay,
Was not apparent; as endearing
As ever, she tripped down the flight
Of stairs, to our poor singer's sight
Like wisp of vagrant hope appearing,
Impulsive, frivolous, and glad,
Exactly as she always had.

VI. 14

"Last night you were so quick to leave us!"
Were the first words that Olga said;
And Lensky, all his soul in grievous
Upheaval, dumbly hung his head.
His jealousy, his rancor, vanished
At that serene regard, were banished
Before that candor, free of art,
That dear simplicity of heart . . .
And lost in sweet enchantment, clearly
He sees he is beloved still;
Pierced by remorse, he shortly will
Ask her forgiveness, waiting merely
For his uncertain tongue to yield
The words; he's happy, all but healed . . .

(VI. 15, 16)

VI. 17

Then starts again to brood and lower;
Yet in his Olga's cheering sight
He finds it is beyond his power
To question her about last night.
He thinks: "I will be her redeemer,
Will not permit the shameless schemer
With sighs and praise and sultry art
To tempt the inexperienced heart,
That noisome gnawing worm shan't slither
Near the young lily's tender stem
Oozing his poison, to condemn
The yet half-open bud to wither."
And all this meant was, in the end:
I shall be shooting at my friend.

VI. 18

Had he but known what secret passion
Was searing poor Tatyana's mind!
Had Tanya gathered in some fashion,
Had she but distantly divined
That shortly in a misty meadow
The two would court the graveyard shadow,
The power of her love, who knows,
Might yet have reconciled the foes.
But no one hitherto suspected
By what emotion she was stirred;
Onegin had not breathed a word,
And Tanya sorrowed undetected.
None but her nanny might have guessed,
And she was slow-witted at best.

VI. 19

He spent the evening in a fluster,
Now darkly taciturn, now bright;
But then, he whom the Muses foster
Is always so; at times he might
Sit down abstracted for a minute,
Strike random chords upon the spinet,
Then stare at Olga, breathe: "My lot
Is happy, Olga—is it not?"
It's late, though; time to leave now. Smarting
With agony, his heart is wrung.
As to the maiden's hand he clung,
It fairly burst at the sad parting.
She looks at him in wonder, starts:
"What is it?" "Nothing." He departs.

VI. 20

Back at the manor, he inspected
His pistols, closed the case; then turned,
Undressed, to Schiller and selected
A volume while the candle burned.
But one concern, in sadness steeping
His heart, dispelled all thought of sleeping:
Olga's fair image, hers alone,
In more than earthly beauty shone
Before his eyes. The Schiller, slighted,
Recedes; he grasps his pen; forth throbs
His verse full-charged with lovelorn sobs,
In tuneful flood. And he recited,
His pent-up lyric surge released,
Like Delvig[2] tipsy at a feast.

VI. 21

By chance these verses did not wither
With him; I have them; thus they go:
"Days of my springtime, whither, whither
Have you withdrawn your golden glow?
What bodes my noonday in its passage?
In vain my glances probe its message,
Deep mist has veiled it from my sight.
No matter; Fate's decree is right.
And if I perish, overtaken
By its swift arrow, or am spared,
All is for good; there is prepared
A time to sleep, a time to waken;
Blessed is the day's laborious tread,
And blessed the dusk when day has fled.

VI. 22

"When with the morrow's ray of dawning
New day will shed its brilliant light,
I may be lead beneath the awning
Of Death's unfathomable night;
The poet's name, it will be buried
In Lethe's lazy stream and ferried
To swift oblivion. Will it fade
As fast for you, oh, beauty's maid,
Or will my early grave be sated
By your fond tears, and will you own:
He loved me, and to me alone
His stormy dawn was dedicated
That turned to night. Dear heart, dear all,
Your spouse awaits; come, heed my call!"

VI. 23

And thus he mourned; we call Romantics
Bards of this dark and languid strain.
(Though how this name describes such antics
I cannot see; but why explain?)
Not long before the dawn was shining,
We see his tired head reclining
Upon the fashion-word "ideal,"
And dreamless sleep upon him steal;
But hardly slumber had enthralled him,
Into the silent chamber broke
Zaretsky's voice and he awoke
As urgently his neighbor called him:
"Past six! Get up, it's time to go.
He'll be already there, you know!"

VI. 24

But he was wrong; for in his chamber
Onegin sleeps, dead to the world.
While cocks are hailing Hesper's amber
And softly night's gray veils are furled,
He slumbers blissfully and deeply.
By now the sun has risen steeply,
A passing blizzard's flakes curvet
In whirling crystal gusts; and yet
Eugene rests safe behind his curtain,
And Morpheus hovers overhead.
At last he rises in his bed
And lifts the drapings to make certain;
He looks, and quickly comes to know
He should have started long ago.

VI. 25

In haste he rings the bell. In hurries
His man, a Frenchman named Guillot,
Lays out his underlinen, scurries
With gown and slippers to and fro.
Onegin lost no moment dressing,
Meanwhile upon his man impressing
To be prepared with proper trim
And pistol-case to drive with him.
The sleigh waits; they get in. Already
They're cantering to the mill, arrive.
Onegin bids the groom to drive
Downfield and hold the horses steady,
His man to carry in his tracks
Lepage's[3] lethal artifacts.

VI. 26

Vladimir had been tensely waiting,
Propped up against the mill-dam here,
Zaretsky learnedly berating
The millstone, rustic engineer.
Apologies. Zaretsky beckoned
And asked, amazed: "But where's your second?"
He worshiped method; to the core
A classicist in duel lore,
Prim and pedantic like a schoolbook,
He did his best to see his man
Rubbed out in style and by the plan
Demanded in the hoary rulebook;
He kept tradition simon-pure
(And merits all our praise, I'm sure).

VI. 27

"My second?" asked Eugene with unction,
"He's here: my friend, Monsieur Guillot.
And I have not the least compunction
To introduce him to you so.
Although he is outshone by many,
He is as fine a lad as any."
Zaretsky chewed his lip, perplexed.
Onegin turned to Lensky next:
"Well, ready?" "Ready." Each departed
Behind the mill to take his stand.
While some way off, Zaretsky and
His colleague, the "fine lad," have started
A grave discussion, the two foes
With lowered eyes maintain their pose.

VI. 28

Foes! Has it been so long a season
That each the other's death prepared?
Long since, at one in act and reason,
In play, at table, they have shared
Each other's lives? And now, indignant,
Like lifelong enemies, malignant,
As in some dreadful, senseless dream,
We see them fiercely, coldly scheme
Each other's doom. . . . Lest either spatter
His hand with blood, might laughter heal
This madness, might a friend's appeal
Yet amiably resolve the matter?
But sham convention works its spell,
Weird honor heeds it all too well.

VI. 29

Now pistols are already gleaming,
Here clash together rods and locks,
Now down the barrels' polished reaming
Descend the balls; here click the cocks.
Down sift the powder's grayish crystals
Upon the pan; lodged in the pistols,
The jagged flint awaits the blow.
Beneath a tree nearby, Guillot
Took up his stand in apprehension.
The foes doffed cloaks. Zaretsky drew
The lines an even thirty-two
Paces apart, with rapt attention.
Across the full allotted space,
They clutch their pistols, face to face.

VI. 30

"Ready—approach!" And coldly glancing
Across the distance at this sign,
With hard and level calm advancing,
They took four steps beyond the line,
Pistols at ease—four fateful paces.
His stride unchanged, Onegin traces
A slow arc with his pistol hand;
They walk five paces farther, and
Lensky, too, starts, his left eye blinking,
To raise his pistol to the aim,
But there—a sudden spurt of flame,
Eugene has fired. His pistol sinking,
The poet reels without a word;
The bell tolls out his term, unheard;

VI. 31

In silence to his bosom raising
A hand, he took no other breath,
And sank, and fell. Opaquely glazing,
His eyes expressed not pain, but death.
So, gently down the slope subsiding,
A sparkling sheet of snow comes sliding.
His heart with sudden chill congealed,
Onegin flew across and kneeled
Beside the boy . . . stared . . . called . . . No answer:
He is not there. Our youthful friend
Has gone to his untimely end.
Becalmed the storm; by searing cancer
Spring's lovely blossom withered lies;
The altar fire grows dim and dies.

VI. 32

Quite still and strangely placid seeming,
He lay in deathly torpor swooned,
His breast pierced through and through, and steaming,
The lifeblood trickled from his wound.
Let time turn back a single minute:
This heart felt transports seethe within it
Of aspiration, love, and strife,
It throbbed with blood, it pulsed with life:
Now the last stir, last sound is uttered,
Like an abandoned house it will
Stay bare and dark, forever still,
Its every window tightly shuttered
And daubed with lime; the mistress fair
Gone without trace, no telling where.

VI. 33

It's fun with witty taunts and sallies
To madden an unwary foe,
It's fun to watch him as he rallies
To gore you like a buffalo,
Yet not without some furtive glaring
Into the mirror, as if daring
His own face. More fun if at once
He bellows "Libel!" like a dunce.
More fun still, to allot this figure
A box six feet below the ground,
Step ritual paces, turn around,
Aim at the pale brow, pull the trigger . . .
To send him to his fathers, though,
Is poorer fun, I'll have you know.

VI. 34

What if your pistol-shot has shattered
The temple of a dear young boy,
Who, flushed with drinking, may have scattered
Rash words at random to annoy,
Sly looks or inadvertent slander;
Or has himself in sudden dander
Incontinently called you out:
I dare say there is little doubt
Your feelings on the point would differ
On that chill dawn when he is found,
Death on his brow, upon the ground,
When, cold already, growing stiffer,
Before your starting eyes he sprawls,
Quite deaf to your despairing calls!

VI. 35

In his clenched fist the pistol grasping,
His heart with rueful anguish filled,
Onegin looked at Lensky, gasping.
"That's that," his neighbor said, "he's killed."
Killed! By the awesome exclamation
Pierced through, Eugene in trepidation
Departs the scene to summon aid.
Into the sleigh Zaretsky laid
The lifeless form, already rigid,
And drove his dreadful burden home.
His horses, broken out in foam
Upon the death-scent, snort and fidget;
Their bits of iron flecked with white,
They speed like arrows in their flight.

VI. 36

My friends, you will lament the poet
Who, flowering with a happy gift,
Must wilt before he could bestow it
Upon the world, yet scarce adrift
From boyhood's shore. Now he will never
Seethe with that generous endeavor,
Those storms of mind and heart again,
Audacious, tender, or humane!
Stilled now are love's unruly urges,
The thirst for knowledge and for deeds,
Contempt for vice and what it breeds,
And stilled you too, ethereal surges,
Breath of a transcendental clime,
Dreams from the sacred realm of rhyme!

VI. 37

Perchance the world would have saluted
In him a savior or a sage;
That lyre of his, forever muted,
Might have resounded down the age
In ceaseless thunder, and have fated
Its bearer to be elevated
To high rank on the worldly grade;
Or haply with his martyred shade
Some holy insight will they bury,
A gem, who knows, of wisdom choice,
Now perished with his living voice.
The hymn of ages will not carry
Deep into his sepulchral den
The benedictions of all men.

(VI. 38)

VI. 39

Or we might guess with equal reason
A fate of far more common cast
For our poet, once the season
Of effervescent youth had passed.
The flame within him would have faltered;
Deep in the country, greatly altered,
He'd live in wedded bliss and horned,
In quilted robe, the Muses scorned.
There he would learn life's essence truly,
By forty would contract the gout,
Would eat and drink, be dull, grow stout,
Sicken, and on his own couch, duly
Wreathed in his offspring, would have died,
While doctors fussed and women cried.

VI. 40

But futile, reader, to uncover
What once his future might have held—
Dead lies our dim young bard and lover,
By friendly hand and weapon felled.
Near where the Muse's ward resided,
Turn left: There is a place provided,
Twin firs grow there, with roots entwined,
And underneath them, freshets wind
That water the adjacent valley.
There girls replenish by the path
Their ringing pitchers at the math,
And there the plowhands like to rally.
There, where the shaded waters lilt,
A simple monument is built.

VI. 41

There, as the rains of spring are wetting
New herbs, the shepherd of the fen,
His shoe of bast with color plaiting,
Will sing of Volga fishermen;
Or a young city lady, spending
A country summer, may be bending
Aside, as on a lonely ride
She roams the meadows far and wide;
Rein in her charging horse before it,
And tugging at the leather strap,
Brush back the veil atop her cap;
Her roving glances will explore it,
And at the simple legend here
Her gentle eye will shed a tear.

VI. 42

Then, at a walk, across the stubble
Her mount will amble from that spot,
And long her mind in rueful trouble
Will meditate on Lensky's lot
And wonder: "Olga, on the morrow . . .
Did she repine in endless sorrow?
Or was the tearful season short?
And Olga's sister . . . ? What report
About the drama's other player,
Of where that sullen hermit dwells,
That modish foe of modish belles,
The youthful poet's freakish slayer?"
I promise, when the time is due
I will report it all to you,

VI. 43

But not at once. However dearly
I prize the hero of my tale,
And though I shall rejoin him, clearly,
Just now my love's a little stale.
The years to somber prose entreat us,
The years dispel the impish meters,
And these, I own it with some rue,
More haltingly I now pursue,
Not with the customary savor
Bedaubs my pen the airy sheets,
Quite other, soberer conceits,
Quite other, sterner cares I favor;
Through silence and through worldly shows
They haunt my dreamy soul's repose.

VI. 44

With new temptations I am lusting,
With yet untasted sorrow sad;
The first I find myself mistrusting,
And hanker for the grief I had.
Oh, dreams, my dreams, where is your sweetness?
Oh, youth's (the rhyme fair beckons) fleetness!
Can it be really true at last,
Its lovely bloom is past, is past,
In truth, in sober earnest ended?
All elegiac pose aside,
The springtime of my days has hied
(As hitherto I just pretended)?
Is it irrevocably noon?
Shall I be really thirty soon?

VI. 45

The afternoon of life is starting,
I see I must confront this truth.
So be it: friendly be our parting,
Oh, nimble season of my youth!
For your delights my thanks I render,
For sufferings, for torments tender,
For turmoil, tempest, revelry,
For all the bounty proffered me
I render thanks. In full, aye, doubled,
Alike in tumult and in calm
I quaffed you, without stint or qualm.
Enough! And now I set, untroubled,
My course for quite another shore
To rest from what I knew before.

VI. 46

One backward glance. Farewell, dear settings
Where my lone days were used to roll,
Instinct with ease and passion's frettings
And musings of the pensive soul.
But you, my verdant inspiration,
Keep ever green imagination,
Come winging oftener to this part;
Come quickening the slumbrous heart,
Let not the poet's soul grow frigid,
Or coarsen to a cruder cast
And turn to lifeless stone at last,
With worldly stupor numb and rigid,
In that vile quicksand where we lie
And wallow, brothers, you and I!

Mikhailovskoye,
1826–27.

Notes

1. "A Parisian restaurateur" ((Pushkin's note).
2. A. Delvig, a contemporary poet and Pushkin's fellow-alumnus of the Lyceum at Tsarskoye Selo.
3. "A famous gunsmith" (Pushkin's note).

*Chapter
Seven*

*Russia's beloved daughter, Moscow,
Where is thy equal to be found?*

DMITRIEV

Not love our Moscow, our own?

BARATYNSKY

*Down Moscow? See the world? Name me a better spot,
Where is it?*

Where we're not.

GRIBOYEDOV

VII. 1

The snows from the surrounding mountains,
By spring's insistent rays beset,
By now cascade in turbid fountains
On meads already glistening wet,
And Nature from her slumber breaking
Greets with a smile the year's awaking.
The sky renews its azure sheen,
And with a downy haze of green
The still transparent forest rallies,
While from her waxen cell the bee
Goes gathering the meadow-fee.
Gay hues invade the drying valleys,
Herds rustle, and the twilight hush
Has thrilled to nightingale and thrush.

VII. 2

How I am saddened by your coming,
Oh, time of love, oh, time of bud!
What languid stir you send benumbing
Into my soul, into my blood!
What painful-tender feeling seizes
The heart, as Spring's returning breezes
Waft to my face in silken rush
Here in the lap of rural hush!
Have I become so alienated
From all things that exult and glow,
All things that joy and life bestow,
That now they find me dull and sated,
And all seems dark as burnt-out coal
To the long-since insentient soul?

VII. 3

Or is it that we are not gladdened
By the renascent leafy gloss
As we remember, wry and saddened,
The bygone autumn's bitter loss?
Perhaps, as Nature freshly burgeons,
We ponder with redoubled urgence
The wilting of our years on earth,
For which there is no gay rebirth;
Or there revives in dreamy glamour,
Once more for us to feel and know,
Another spring of long ago
And sends our heartstrings in a tremor
With glimpses of a distant shore,
A magic moon that shines no more . . .

VII. 4

Springtime! Epicurean sages,
Dear lazybones of every hue,
And you, bucolic Levshin's[1] pages,
Bland-tempered fortunates, and you,
Provincial Priams fed on lentil,
And gentlewomen sentimental:
Spring calls you to the countryside,
It's basking, blooming, planting tide,
The season of enraptured strolling,
Of languidly seductive nights.
Come, faster, friends, you should by rights
In crowded stage or chaise be rolling
Past city gate and bar, and out
Into the open fields about.

VII. 5

You also, kindly reader, ready
Your foreign chaise, abandon too
The city fevered and unsteady,
Where you caroused the winter through.
Come, hark, my errant muse beside us,
The leafy sough; and she will guide us
Toward the stream without a name,
Back to that country seat, the same
Where my Eugene, vain recluse laden
With vain ennui, was known to stay
But lately, and not far away
Tanya, my dear, my dreamy maiden—
Which now stands vacant and bereft
But for the trail of grief he left.

VII. 6

By rolling mountains half-surrounded,
Come, let us wander where one sees
A brook meander, meadow-bounded,
Across a grove of linden trees.
Night-long, the nightingale, spring's lover,
Sings there, and heather roses hover
Above the coursing water's drone;
And here a tomb and graven stone—
Two venerable firs impart it
Their shadow—tell the passing guest:
"Vladimir Lensky here found rest,
Who met death young and eager-hearted;
Such was the year, *so long* his lease.
Fair youth and poet, sleep in peace."

VII. 7

There, for a time, when night had ended,
On a low branch one might discern
A wreath, by unknown hand suspended,
Asway above the tranquil urn;
And for a time, two maidens yonder
At leisured eventide would wander
And by the rising moon be found
In mingled tears upon the mound.
But now . . . the mournful shrine is never
Sought out; the trail that passed beneath,
Untrod; the fir-branch bears no wreath.
Alone the shepherd sings as ever,
Grizzled and frail, his simple air
And plaits his artless sandal there.

(VII. 8, 9)

VII. 10

Ah, hapless Lensky! Youthful sorrows
Do not endure, its tears are brief;
It took the bride but few tomorrows
To be unfaithful to her grief.
Another managed to engage her
Fond thoughts, another to assuage her
Bereavement with a fresh love's balm;
An uhlan snared her with his charm,
An uhlan won her heart's devotion . . .
And here already see her stand
In bridal wreath to join her hand
To his, all maidenly emotion,
Her lowered eyes on fire, while
Her lips curve in a heedless smile.

VII. 11

Ah, hapless Lensky! Where you linger
In yonder timeless deaf retreat,
Say, were you saddened, mournful singer,
By the dread news of her deceit?
Or does he drift down Lethe's healing
Dream currents, blissfully unfeeling,
Beyond all sorrow's reach, the world
Forever stilled to him and furled?
It must be so! Oblivion lonely
Awaits our shadows down below,
The tones of lover, friend, and foe
Are silenced all at once, and only
The angry heirs to our estate
Intone their scandalous debate.

VII. 12

And all too soon in Larin Manor
Young Olga's tuneful voice was stilled;
Her groom was due to join his banner,
Slave to his lot, like all his guild.
Farewells: the aged mother, streaming
With tears, clung to her daughter, seeming
With bitter grief quite overcome;
Tatyana, though, was strangely numb
And dry-eyed, though a pallor mortal
Had overcast her stricken face,
When, crowding for a last embrace
Around the carriage at the portal,
They parted from the bridal pair.
She saw them off, and lingering there,

VII. 13

She watched them dwindle for an endless
Moment as through a blur of tears . . .
And here she was, alone and friendless!
Companion of so many years,
Alas! her darling spoilt and cherished,
Endeared from birth and jointly nourished,
Was carried far beyond her ken,
And never to be seen again.
And wayward like a shadow, grieving
Into the empty park she strays,
No place or thing to cheer the gaze;
Turn where she would, there's no relieving
The tears that smother her unspent,
And all the while her heart is rent.

VII. 14

Harsh solitude makes more insistent
Her passion's flame and fans it more,
And of Onegin, now so distant,
Her heart speaks louder than before.
She cannot hope to see him ever,
And for her brother's death should sever
All traffic with his slayer. True,
The poet's slain and gone; but who
Here in the world he left still felt it?
His bride so soon re-wed and flown,
His image swiftly faded, blown
Like smoke into the sky and melted.
Two hearts, perhaps, for his sad lot
Were grieving still . . . grieving for what?

VII. 15

Dusk gathered gently. In the gloaming
Calm waters coursed. A beetle whirred.
Field crews, their round-songs stilled, were homing.
Smoke rose across the river, stirred
From winking fishers' fires. Hillward,
Across the empty fields that, silvered,
Beneath the dreamy moonlight shone,
Tatyana wandered long alone,
Bemused; until the hilltop brought her
Close on a hamlet at her feet:
A copse downhill, a country seat,
A park sloped to the shining water.
She looked—and quickened pulses smote
Their heavy drumbeat at her throat.

VII. 16

She stands perplexed, and doubts befall her:
"Go boldly on? Turn on the spot?
But he's not here. Just as a caller
I'll see the house, that park . . . Why not?"
Uneasily the girl advances,
Downhill and, barely breathing, glances
About with wondering regard . . .
And enters the deserted yard.
Dogs rush at her with bark and bustle;
Alerted by her startled shout,
Serf boys and girls from near about
Come running. Not without a tussle,
They keep the frisking dogs at bay,
Escorting the young miss away.

VII. 17

"Is one allowed to see the manor?"
Inquired Tatyana. In response
The children ran for Mistress Anna
And carried word to her. At once
The chatelaine emerged who wielded
Those idle keys. The hall-door yielded,
And Tanya let her glances roam
What lately was our hero's home:
A laid-up billiard cue still rested
Across the table after play;
There on a rumpled sofa lay
A riding crop. Onward she quested;
"This fireplace," pointed out the crone,
"Here Master used to sit alone.

VII. 18

"And here he sat in winter, dining
With neighbor Lensky, frequent guest
Until his death; and here, adjoining,
His study. Here he used to rest,
Receive the bailiff who reported
On the estate; here he resorted
For morning coffee or a book . . .
Old master also liked this nook:
On Sundays he might take his station
Here by the window, don his specs
And play with me at Sixty-six.
The Good Lord grant his soul salvation
And his poor bones a peaceful berth
In the cool lap of mother earth!"

VII. 19

Tatyana, moved and wonder-stricken,
Feasts on it all with dreamy eyes,
And ache with solace mingled quicken
The languid heart, each sight a prize
More dear than treasure-trove of fable:
His lamp, now dark, upon the table,
The rows of books, the carpet spread
Beneath the window on his bed,
The hazy moonshot view, the solemn
Half-light diffused about the room,
Lord Byron's portrait in the gloom,
The statuette upon its column,
Hat over knitted forehead pressed,
Arms folded tight across the chest[2]

VII. 20

Spellbound, Tatyana mused and lingered
Within that modern hermit's cell.
At last the mists of evening fingered
The river dale, and darkness fell
Where grove and sleepy waters blended;
The moon behind the hills descended
Before our fair young pilgrim found
She should long since be homeward bound.
Repressing any exhibition
Of feeling, save a single sigh,
Tatyana turned to say good-by,
But first requested free permission
To use the anchorite's late lair
To do some private reading there.

VII. 21

Beyond the gate Tatyana parted
From the appointed chatelaine;
Come dawn next day, though, she had started
For the abandoned hall again.
There, in the silence of the study,
Remote at last from everybody,
All else forgotten for the nonce,
She stood forlorn, and all at once
In tears ... At length, still half-unheeding,
Upon those books she turned her mind,
And finding them of curious kind,
She soon was all engrossed in reading,
An eager passage, door on door,
To worlds she never knew before.

VII. 22

We know Eugene had turned from fiction
And earnest reading with contempt;
But from his sweeping interdiction
Some works had always been exempt—
The bard of *Don Juan* and *Giaour*,
And certain novels[3] with a power
To focus and reflect the age,
Where shown upon the current stage,
Man moves with truth and animation:
Unprincipled, perversely bent
Upon himself, his talents spent
In reverie and speculation,
With his exacerbated mind
In idle seething self-confined.

VII. 23

There were preserved on many pages
Sharp traces of a fingernail;
Each such memorial engages
Her close attention without fail.
Tatyana notes with trepidation
By what idea or observation
Onegin's mind was strongly moved,
Or what he silently approved.
In penciled marginal notations
She finds Onegin's heart unsealed;
On every page there are revealed
Involuntary intimations
Of where he nodded or demurred
With query, cross, or scribbled word.

VII. 24

And step by step my Tanya, learning
His mind, at last begins to see
The man for whom she has been yearning
By willful destiny's decree
More clearly than by face and feature:
A strangely bleak and reckless creature,
Issue of Heaven or of Hell,
Proud demon, angel—who can tell?
Perhaps he is all imitation,
An idle phantom or, poor joke,
A Muscovite in Harold's cloak,
An alien whim's interpretation,
Compound of every faddish pose. . . ?
A parody, perhaps . . . who knows?

VII. 25

Has she, by any chance, detected
The missing *key*, unlocked the door?
Time flies, though; she has been expected
At home these many hours before.
There neighbor-folk are congregated
And Tanya's conduct is debated.
"Tatyana's grown now . . . what to do?"
Wheezed the old lady to those two.
"Here's Olga gone; Tanya's the older,
Time she were settled too, but there—
I don't know what to do with her;
To everything that I have told her,
It's been 'I won't'; it's mope and moan,
And roaming in the woods alone."

VII. 26

"Is she in love, perhaps?" "I wonder
With whom? Buyanov she refused;
With Petyushkov, the selfsame blunder;
Pykhtin of the Hussars, he used
To stay with us, and was he ever
Struck with Tatyana—wild to have her!
I had my fingers crossed, but then,
Bah! Nothing came of it again."
"But my dear lady, need I say it?
To Moscow, to the marriage fair!
The trade is always brisker there."
"The money, though! How would I pay it?"
"One winter you can manage, come!
Come worst to worst, I'll lend you some."

VII. 27

The shrewd old lady saw good reason
To heed such sapient advice,
And soon resolved to spend the season
In Moscow, having weighed the price.
But Tanya, hearing this disclosure,
Dreads to envisage the exposure
To a sophisticated gaze
Of her unspoilt provincial ways,
Of her unfashionable dresses,
Unfashionable repartee!
How face the mocking scrutiny
Of Moscow swanks and lionesses?
She'd die! Far better to have been
Confined in her dear, dull demesne.

VII. 28

She slips outdoors upon the morrow
At the first aureole of light,
And with a gaze of love and sorrow
Encompassing the cherished sight,
Whispers: Calm valleys where I sauntered,
Farewell; lone summits that I haunted,
Beloved forest groves, good-by;
Farewell, dear jewel of the sky,
Farewell, all Nature gay and tender,
From your still haven I am hurled
Into an idly glittering world—
Dear freedom that I must surrender,
Good-by! Where is my path to lead?
What has my destiny decreed?

VII. 29

And ever longer does she ramble;
A mountain stream, a knoll or dell
Will beckon her to stop or amble
More slowly in its quiet spell;
And restlessly we find her darting
Through field and wood, as if departing
From dear companions of the past.
But fleeting summer dwindles fast
To golden autumn, Nature trembling,
For all her gorgeous state, in dread,
Wreathed victim to the altar led . . .
The northern wind has blown, assembling
Its cloudy hosts in rage, and lo—
The fairy winter reigns below.

VII. 30

She came in powdery whirls, her tresses
Entwined among the oaken boughs,
In silky silver blankets dresses
The meadow folds and mountain brows,
The river's rough embankments smoothing
With downy drapes, its current soothing
In shells of ice. She makes us gay
With her exuberant display—
All but Tatyana, who is shrinking
From dashing at the bathhouse roof
Pure snow on face and breast, aloof
From winter rites, slow to be drinking
The coldly scintillating air:
This winter's entry frightens her.

VII. 31

Departure day at last approaches,
Twice missed before and reassigned;
The long-neglected travel coach is
Inspected, mended, newly lined.
The usual train: three wagons rattle
With various domestic chattel,
With chairs and chests, and pots and pans,
With mattresses and quilts, and cans
Of jelly, cockerels in cages,
With basins, dishes, crocks and jars,
And sundry odd etceteras.
And now the serf-hall wails and rages
With valedictory distress,
As eighteen jaded hacks, no less,

VII. 32

They lead into the yard and fasten
To harness; ever higher loom
The piled-up carts, the scullions hasten
To ready breakfast, wench and groom
Trade shouts. The rough postillion urges
His rough nag; at the gate converges
The servant company in strength
To bob and scrape good-by. At length
They're settled in their seats, and slowly
The portly sleigh-coach gathers way.
"Farewell, calm scenes, it's time to say
Farewell, my refuge lone and lowly!
Forever . . . ?" And in headlong rush
The tears from Tanya's lashes gush.

VII. 33

When by-and-by this country's borders
Relent to blest enlightenment
(The Philosophic Charts accord us
Five hundred years for this event),
Then certainly our roads' condition
Will change beyond all recognition:
Majestic highways will connect
Points far and near, and intersect
Throughout the realm. Rude fords and runnels
By iron bridges will be spanned,
We shall move mountains overland,
Pierce riverbeds with callous tunnels;
Civilization then, one feels,
May even run to roadside meals.

VII. 34

Our highways now are hard on coaches,
Our bridges mold in disrepair;
At stationhouses, bugs and roaches
Drive weary travelers to despair;
Meals are a myth. The would-be spender
Finds menus whose linguistic splendor
Masks utter culinary gloom
Hung in a chilly waiting room
To taunt him. Rude cyclopes bustle
At sluggish forges, bent to heal
The wingèd European wheel
With Scythian hammer-blow and muscle,
And bless amid their clumsy toil
The potholes of the native soil.

VII. 35

By contrast, in the wintry season
One slithers pleasantly along
On tracks as smooth and bare of reason
As lyrics in a modern song.
Our charioteers are keen and able,
Our troikas indefatigable,
And miles, to cheer the idle gaze,
Flash past like fenceposts in a haze.
Worse luck, Tatyana's mother wasted
No cash on horses for relay,
But took the home team all the way,
And our luckless damsel tasted
Full measure of the joys I praise:
They traveled fully seven days.

VII. 36

The goal drew near. Before them, raising
Their whitestone pinnacles, with streaks
Of golden crosses fiercely blazing,
Loom Moscow's venerable peaks.
Oh, how my heart would leap, good people,
As church and palace, park and steeple
In sweeping, marvelous array
Fanned out and took my breath away!
How often in my cheerless erring
Afar from here, in bitter rue,
My Moscow, have I thought of you!
Moscow . . . All strings are set to stirring
In Russian hearts by that dear knell!
What worlds of meaning in it dwell!

VII. 37

First, rising from its oak grove yonder,
They see Tsar Peter's Palace[4] frown,
And somberly it seems to ponder
Its recent ominous renown.
In vain Napoleon awaited,
By his last feats intoxicated,
Moscow in homage on her knees
To yield the ancient Kremlin's keys.
No—Moscow did not bow its hoary
Crown, but prepared a gift of hate,
A flaming holocaust, to fête
The hero waiting in his glory!
And forthwith, sunk in pensive gloom,
He gazed into his fiery doom.

VII. 38

Farewell now, scene of grandeur humbled,
Petrovsky Palace; onward, fast!
And presently the carriage rumbled
Toward the shining tollgate; past
The barrier, and on it hobbles
Across Tverskaya's holes and cobbles,
Past shops and lanterns, crones and youths,
By convents, gardens, mansions, booths,
Bokharans, sleighs, muzhiks in blouses,
By cossacks, merchants, kitchen yards,
Past battlements and boulevards,
Parks, pharmacies, and fashion houses,
Past gates where guardian lions rear,
While daws about the crosses veer.

(VII. 39)

VII. 40

In this way, travel-worn and shaken,
They spend an hour and still move on;
At last the slowing coach has taken
A turn-off by St. Chariton
And stopped. For here they will be quartered
At an old cousin's, sadly martyred
By slow consumption these four years.
The door is opened, through it peers
A ragged white-thatched kalmyk, plying
His darning needles. They are shown
Into the drawing room, where prone
Upon her couch, the princess, crying
In wonder, offers her embrace;
And tears and questions flow apace.

VII. 41

"Princess, *mon ange!*" "Pachette!" "Alina!"
"Who could ..." "Dear cousin, all these years!"
"It's ages, child, I haven't seen her ..."
"Sit down—I'm so amazed, my dears,
No flight of fiction could be bolder!"
"This is Tatyana, ma'am, my older ..."
"Why, Tanya, let me look at you!
I must be dreaming—is it true?
Your Grandison, do you remember? ..."
"What Grandison? ... Oh, *Grandison!*
Yes, yes, of course ... Where has he been?"
"Why, here; St. Simeon's. Last December
He called on me, on Christmas Eve.
His son got married, I believe.

VII. 42

"And he . . . but all our news had better
Be told another time. Oh, yes!
Tanya's relations have not met her;
We'll call tomorrow. I confess,
I can't present you as required,
Can scarcely move . . . But you are tired,
Let's all go in and take a rest.
How weak I am . . . my poor old chest . . .
As I am now, I'm hardly fitter
For joy than sorrow. Ah, my dear,
I'm good for nothing now, I fear;
The trials of old age are bitter . . ."
Here the poor sufferer broke off
And feebly wept, racked by her cough.

VII. 43

The invalid's kind words and kisses
Did touch Tatyana; nonetheless
She feels uneasy here and misses
Her room with all its homeliness.
These silken drapes seem to encumber
Her weary limbs and fend off slumber;
By dawn the sounds of many bells—
The morning labor's herald knells—
Are hardly needed to arouse her.
The prospect from her window yields
No cheering vista of her fields,
For all this city room allows her
By way of slowly brightening views
Are fences, sculleries, and mews.

VII. 44

So from one luncheon to another
They haul Tatyana day by day,
To mother's mother, aunt, and brother
Her listless languor to display.
Their kin, arrived from such a distance,
Is wined and dined with fond persistence
And treated to a steady drone:
"My word, Tatyana, how you're grown!
It seems last year that you were christened!"
"I dandled you when you were small!"
"I had to cuff you, I recall . . ."
"You loved my seedcakes!" And she listened
To aunts in chorus everywhere:
"How time does fly, I do declare!"

VII. 45

Yet here, time's fleeting passage never
Stirs the unalterable rule:
Old aunt Yelena wears as ever
The same old bonnet trimmed with tulle;
The powder on Lukerya Lvovna,
The fibs of dear Lyubov Petrovna
Are still as thick as they were once;
Ivan Petrovich's still a dunce
His brother still a money-grubber,
Aunt Pelya still keeps at her house
Her friend Finemouche, her spitz, her spouse,
Who's still a faithful English-Clubber,
As deaf and meek as e'er he was,
And eats and drinks without a pause.

VII. 46

Their daughters welcomed with embraces
The cousin fresh from out-of-town,
And then those youthful Moscow Graces
In silence looked her up and down,
And in her bearing they detected
Something provincial and affected,
They found her somewhat pale and small,
But quite attractive, all in all.
Then familiarity progresses,
As girlish nature takes its course:
They kiss her, squeeze her hand, perforce
Fluff up-to-style Tatyana's tresses,
And soon their cherished secrets all
Come pouring in a singsong drawl;

VII. 47

Their dreams and conquests, hopes exalted
Or dashed, are sweetly dwelt upon,
And, with a pinch of slander salted,
Their artless prattle gushes on;
And then they coaxingly command her
To pay them back with equal candor,
Unburdening her own heart's freight.
But Tanya, in a dreamlike state,
Has scarcely heard their fond effusions,
Not understanding any part;
The sacred cargo of her heart,
Its store of tears and blest illusions,
She keeps inviolate and whole,
And will not share it with a soul.

VII. 48

She would avoid their empty patter,
Rejoin the company—in vain:
The parlor offers only chatter,
All desultory and inane,
So incoherent, smug, and jointless,
Their very calumnies seem pointless;
In all that chaff of stale remarks
Trite questions, gossip, news, there sparks
No wit from one day to another,
If but unwittingly; long since
The arid heart has ceased to wince
Or feign, the sluggish mind to bother
With fun. What world so drably vile
Its follies even draw no smile!

VII. 49

Young Archivists[5] in rows and clusters
Appraised her with their fishlike stare,
And later in their private musters
Her notices were less than fair.
One droopy sort of fool contended
She was "ideal to earth descended,"
And penned against a lacquered jamb
An elegiac epigram.
At some dull auntie's, it transpired,
Prince Vyazemsky sat down a while
By her and managed to beguile
Her mind; and seeing her so squired,
Some ancient with his wig askew
Was moved to ask if someone knew . . . ?

VII. 50

But where Melpomene's fine raving
Reverberates both long and loud,
Where her bedizened drapes are waving
Before a less-than-frenzied crowd,
Where dear Thalia's gently napping,
Deaf to her champions' friendly clapping,
Where youth reserves exclusive fee
Of worship to Terpsichore
(As was the case, too, when we knew her,
When you and I were youngsters yet)—
No lady's rancorous lorgnette
Was even once directed to her,
Nor dandies' double-barreled stares
From boxes or proscenium chairs.

VII. 51

To the Assembly, too, they drag her,
Where hubbub, heat, the music's gale,
The whirling couples' swish and swagger
The senses all at once assail;
The ladies' airy dresses gleaming,
The galleries astir and teeming,
That all-encircling *cour de dames,*
Conspire to dazzle and to numb.
Here stalks the veteran fop, parading
His careless spyglass, swank *gilet,*
And his habitual *toupet,*[6]
Here flock hussars on leave, invading
This one-night stage, to bluster on,
To glitter, conquer, and be gone.

VII. 52

Bright stars bejewel the darkling ether,
Bright beauties star the Moskva's strand;
All constellations dim beneath her,
The Moon outshines their spangled band.
Thus she, to whom my timid lyre
Is not presuming to aspire,[7]
Like the resplendent moon does throne
Among the maidens, bright alone.
How proud in radiance she advances,
Her feet afloat upon the ground!
What ardor at her breast is found!
What wondrous languor in her glances! . . .
But stay—not once before you raved,
Not once succumbed, and were enslaved.

VII. 53

Galop, mazurka, waltz, gay welter
Of noise and bustle, bobbed and swerved,
While by a column, in her shelter
Of aunts, Tatyana, unobserved,
Looked on unseeingly and pondered
In shy distaste; her spirit wandered
Far from this boisterous affair,
Far from its sultry, sullied air,
Back home toward those lowly hovels,
That pastoral sequestered nook
A-murmur with its limpid brook,
Back to her flowers and to her novels,
Those linden-shaded walks, the same
Down one of which, one day, *he* came.

VII. 54

Thus worlds away her thoughts are straying,
The crowd, the ball become a blur,
While here a general, grave and graying,
Can't seem to take his eyes off her;
When aunt has winked at aunt and nodded,
Tatyana from each side is prodded
And hears a whisper in each ear:
"Look quickly, on your left, my dear!"
"My left? What is it? All I see is . . ."
"Well, look, whatever it may be . . ."
There, in that group at left, you see
Two other officers where he is . . .
Now you can see him! No, you can't . . ."
"Not that stout general, my aunt?"

VII. 55

But here, with bows before this feather
In Tanya's cap, we turn away,
Lest we abandon altogether
The one I sing, and go astray . . .
Yes—let me quickly put on record:
I sing of a young friend, his checkered
Career in fortune's cruel coil.
Thy blessing on my earnest toil,
O Epic Muse! About me hover,
And ever lend thy faithful wand,
Lest I roam thither and beyond!
That's all, and I am glad it's over,
My debt to classicism paid:
Though late, the Invocation's made.

Moscow, Mikhailovskoye, St. Petersburg, Malinniki,
1827–28.

Notes

1. "Levshin, author of many treatises on husbandry" (Pushkin's note).

2. A statuette of Napoleon.

3. From Pushkin's own library and other evidence it is assumed that the allusion here is to Benjamin Constant's *Adolphe* and possibly other best sellers of the New Sensibility and the age of Rousseau.

4. Petrovsky Palace near Moscow became Napoleon's headquarters when the great fire of 1812 drove him from the city.

5. Young exquisites serving in the Archive Department of the Foreign Office, then evidently thought of as a haven for aesthetes, highbrows, and intellectual snobs.

6. French equivalent of Yiddish *chutzpe*, "impudence, crust." The Russian has *nakhal'stvo*.

7. The senior Russian exegete of *Eugene Onegin*, Brodsky, surmised that this passage apostrophizes Alexandra Korsakova.

*Chapter
Eight*

*Fare thee well, and if for ever,
Still for ever fare thee well.*

BYRON

VIII. 1

When in the parks of the Lyceum
A carefree flower life I led,[1]
And eagerly read *Apuleium*,
But *Ciceronem* left unread,
In springtime, when the stillness brought us
But swan calls over gleaming waters—
In valleys charged with mystery
The Muse began to visit me.
Into my monkish study breaking
Like sudden dawn, she would ignite
Gay fireworks of fancy flight
And sing of childish merrymaking,
Our glorious dawn's heroic themes,
The heart's first palpitating dreams.

VIII. 2

And lo, the public smiled, and served us
The fairy-food of early fame;
Derzhavin in old age observed us
And, grave-bound, with his blessings came . . .[2]

VIII. 3

And I, adopting for sole canons
The passions' arbitrary cues,
Confiding all to chance companions—
I brought my enterprising Muse
To noisy feasts and disputations,
Patrolmen's midnight imprecations,
And at such giddy feasts she flung
Her gifts among the boisterous throng,
A young bacchante—joined their revels
And, singing to the clink of glass,
Was wooed with many an ardent pass
By those now middle-aged young devils;
And I was happy to show off
My volatile young ladylove.

VIII. 4

But angry fortune glared upon me
And drove me far . . . She left me not,
My tender maid, and often won me
Sweet respite with a wondrous plot
That charmed the burden off my shoulders.
How often, 'mid Caucasian boulders
On moonlit gallops it was she
Who, like Lenore, rode with me![3]
How often by the Tauris' waters
She led the way, through misty caves
Of night, to hear the murmuring waves,
The endless lisp of Nereus' daughters,
The breakers' deep, eternal choir
In praise of all creation's sire!

VIII. 5

The capital's ado and glitter
Forsworn as soon as left behind,
She roamed the humble tents of bitter
Moldavia, and found them kind.
In that bleak wilderness she rambled
With wandering tribes, and soon resembled
Her hosts, forgot for their scant tongue
That of the gods whence she had sprung,
And learned the airs of that steppe pleasance.
Then—sudden shift of scene all round—
In my own garden she was found,
Clothed in a country damsel's presence,
In wistful musing steeped her glance,
And in her hand a book from France.

VIII. 6

Now for the first time I am squiring
My Muse to a full-dress soirée,
At once resenting and admiring
Her prairie charms here on display.
Through serried ranks aristocratic,
Sartorial, martial, diplomatic
She glides, now in, now out of sight,
Now, resting, savors with delight
The buzzing, many-headed cluster,
The flash of silky trains and jests,
The slow procession of the guests
By the young hostess passed in muster:
Bright gowns with somber dress suits lined,
Like pictures in black frames confined.

VIII. 7

She likes the stately conversation,
Hierarchically stratified,
The cool assurance of high station
That wealth of rank and years provide.
To this choice circle, who invited
The guest that, silent, as if blighted,
Stands there alone and known to none?
Blank faces pass and hurry on
Like vexing phantoms seen obscurely;
Spleen, or a kind of bleak hauteur
Shows on his face—what brought him there?
Who is he? Not Onegin, surely?
Or is it? . . . Yes, indeed. "And when
Did he return to us again?"

VIII. 8

"And is he mellowed by migration,
Or still the crank he was before?
Tell us, what new impersonation,
What pose is held for us in store?
Well? Cosmopolitan, Melmotic,
Childe Haroldesque or patriotic,
Tartuffe or Quaker, may one ask,
Or yet another faddish mask?
Or will he be like everybody,
Like you and me, just a good egg?
At all events, one thing I beg:
Discard the style that's worn and shoddy,
One tires of the stale old show . . ."
"Why, do you know him?" — "Yes and no."

VIII. 9

Why then attempt to be so clever,
So merciless at his expense?
Because we sit in judgment ever
And pry with ceaseless vigilance?
Because the rash missteps of heroes
Invoke from self-complacent zeros
Resentment or a gloating grin?
Because broad minds hem small ones in?
Or since too often we are willing
To take reported talk for deeds,
And idle spite on dullness feeds,
And pompous men find rubbish thrilling?
Do we feel snugly "in our own"
With mediocrity alone?

VIII. 10

Blest he who, green in adolescence,
Matured at the appointed stage,
Who tasted of life's acrid essence
And learnt to stomach it with age;
Who for strange transports never lusted,
Through worldly slime strode undisgusted,
At twenty was a fop or blade,
At thirty a good marriage made,
At fifty shed by liquidation
All debts, both private and the rest,
And issued painlessly possessed
Of money, rank, and reputation,
And whom you hear throughout his span
Referred to as "an excellent man!"

VIII. 11

But sad to feel, when youth has left us,
That it was given us in vain,
That its unnoticed flight bereft us
And brought no harvest in its train:
That our most fondly nursed ambitions,
Our fancy's freshest apparitions,
Have swiftly wilted one by one,
Like leaves by autumn blasts undone;
To see no prospect but an endless
Array of meals in solemn row,
To watch life like a puppet show,
Do as the Romans do, yet friendless,
And sharing with that titled crew
No single passion, taste, or view.

VIII. 12

Once marked by noisy talk, one really
Gets furious to be set down
By men of better sense as merely
A specimen, half freak, half clown;
Be stuck with a poor half-wit's label
Or thought a ghoul from Satan's stable
Or else that "Demon" of my pen![4]
To take Onegin up again,
When he had killed his friend and neighbor—
Now twenty-six, still vague of aim,
Void of employment—he became
A martyr to his leisure's labor:
No service, business, or wife
To occupy his empty life.

VIII. 13

The travel-fever took possession
Of him, the up-and-going fit
(A most unfortunate obsession,
Though some do volunteer for it).
He left his realm of wood and meadow,
The solitude wherein a shadow,
A blood-bespattered specter fey
Appeared to haunt him every day,
And he embarked on aimless roaming;
To feel was all that he desired. . . .
As of all else, he soon grew tired
Of restlessness, and started homing:
And just like Chatsky,⁵ chanced to fall
From shipboard straight into a ball.

VIII. 14

And presently the crowd divided,
There was a whisper and a stir . . .
A lady to the hostess glided,
A portly general after her.
She was not cold, nor too vivacious,
Not taciturn, nor yet loquacious;
No forward glance or bold address,
No conscious straining for success,
Without affected mannerism
Or specious second-hand conceit—
All calm, all simple, all discreet,
She seemed a living catechism
Du comme il faut (Shishkov, be kind!⁶
This won't translate, so never mind).

VIII. 15

Young ladies flocked to her intently,
And old ones welcomed her with smiles,
Men bowed to her more reverently
And sought her glance across the aisles.
No girl, it seemed, would step as loudly
While passing her; and none more proudly
Raised nose and shoulders in the air
Than he who was her escort there.
One hardly found in her what passes
For beauty, but no more could find
A single blemish of the kind
That London's fashionable classes
In their fastidious slang decry
As *vulgar*. And I vainly try . . .

VIII. 16

I'm very fond of this locution,
But vainly try to render it;
As yet, with us, its distribution
Is small, and it is scarcely fit
For any use but rhyming meanly . . .
Back to our lady, though: serenely,
Unchallengeably sweet and dear,
She was that moment sitting near
The dazzling Nina Voronskaya,[7]
That Cleopatra of our clime;
Yet surely even her sublime
Marmoreal gleam could not aspire
To shine her neighbor out of view,
Although she fairly blinded you.

VIII. 17

"Why, could it be?" Onegin wonders,
"Could it be she? It is! . . . yet what
Could possibly bring *her*," he ponders,
"Out of that god-forsaken spot . . . ?"
The faithful spyglass keeps returning
To her, now doubting, now discerning
Another half-remembered trait.
"Your pardon, Prince, but tell me, pray,
Who is she—there—in conversation
With Spain's envoy—in the purple cap?"
The prince looked puzzled. "My dear chap,
You've long been out of circulation. . . .
I'll introduce you; come, let's go."
"Who is she, then?" "My wife, you know."

VIII. 18

"So you've been married! Why, I owe you
Good wishes! Long?" "Two years or so;
A Larina . . . What? Does she know you?"
"Tatyana! . . . Yes, we're neighbors." "Oh!
We must go over, have you meet her."
And so the prince brought up to greet her
His dear old friend of former days.
She met him with a level gaze . . .
If she was poignantly affected,
If she was shaken or unnerved—
Her calm eyes never flinched or swerved.
Cool, imperturbable, collected,
Her voice in no wise changed in key,
Her bow was easy, gracious, free.

VIII. 19

Amazing! Not the slightest tremor,
Her diction never halts or trips;
No change of color, frown or stammer,
No faint compression of the lips.
For all he labored to detect it,
He found no vestige that connected
This lady with the girl he knew.
He would maneuver for a clue
By conversation, would have spoken
But failed . . . She asked his route and dates,
And had he comes from their estates,
Then sent the prince a glance in token
Of weariness, "would be excused,"
And left him rigid and bemused.

VIII. 20

The girl whom he had gently scolded
Once, far away and tête-à-tête
(Before our tale had quite unfolded),
Whom, like a prim old magistrate,
He had presumed to read a lecture . . .
Who would have ventured to conjecture
That she, who penned in tender youth
That note, all candor and all truth,
Which he still kept, a declaration . . .
That same Tatyana—had he dreamed
All this?—to whom it must have seemed
That he disdained her age and station,
Could face him now without a qualm,
So blandly self-assured and calm?

VIII. 21

And presently, confused and fretful,
He left the tightly packed soirée.
Dreams, now alluring, now regretful,
Pursued him far into the day.
At length he wakened, barely rested,
To find a note: Prince N. requested
The honor of his company
That night. "To see her! Oh, to be
With her! I shall!" In courteous fashion
He scrawls acceptance. What strange trance
Has seized him, what absurd romance
Upset his torpid self-possession?
Hurt pride? Frivolity? Or, bane
And bliss of youngsters, love again?

VIII. 22

Once more Onegin seeks to hurry
The clock, speed on tonight's approach.
Ten strikes, and in unwanted flurry
He's off as soon as in the coach,
Arrives, steps in, his pulses beating,
And fortune grants a private meeting.
Yet, once alone and just across
From her, he flounders, at a loss
For words. An awkward, foolish
Constraint befalls him like a huff:
He sulks and barely speaks enough
For courtesy, sunk in a mulish
Staring dejection; whereas she
Remains superbly poised and free.

VIII. 23

Her husband joins them soon, concluding
The unsuccessful tête-à-tête;
He draws Onegin out, alluding
To pranks and jests of former date.
They laugh; then other guests arrive, and
The party talk is soon enlivened
By the crude salt of worldly spite;
But, with this hostess, it is light,
Gay nonsense, free of priggish preening,
Or, grave at times, is never brought
To fatuous themes or hallowed thought,
But brims with undidactic meaning;
And its high spirits and good sense
Are powerless to give offense.

VIII. 24

Yet these were rank's and fashion's aces,
Who set the tone and make the rules,
Those constantly encountered faces
And those inevitable fools;
Here were those beldames trimmed with roses
In mobcaps and malignant poses,
Here sundry virgins sat in state,
Uncompromisingly sedate;
An envoy here expatiated
Upon some diplomatic theme;
A powdered wag, *ancien régime,*
Here jested with that somewhat dated
Spry mastery of thrust and feint
That now seems just a little quaint.

VIII. 25

Here was the carper, whose fastidious
Wry barbs were hurled with baleful force,
Who damned the sweet tea (too, too hideous),
The ladies (flat), the men's tone (coarse),
That book they all were overrating,
That badge decreed two maids-in-waiting,[8]
The stupid war, those papers rife
With lies, the snow, and his own wife . . .

VIII. 26

Here was Prolasov,[9] ever gaining
From baseness notoriety,
At whom in albums you've been training
And blunting quills galore, St. Priest;
There stood, a fine cartoonist's figure,
Another peerless party-rigger,
Like a Palm-Sunday cherub flushed,
Tight-corseted, unmoving, hushed.
Some traveler back from distant places
An overstarched young jackanapes,
Attracted many smiles and gapes
By his pretentious airs and graces,
And mutely, eyes would meet and skim
Aside in obloquy of him.

VIII. 27

Meanwhile, Eugene was vainly thrusting
Tatyana's image from his mind:
Not of poor shy Tatyana—trusting,
In love, obscure, and unrefined,
But of the princess who serenely,
Like sheltered godhead, ruled the queenly
The lush imperial Nevá.
Ah, men! The curse of Eve, our far
Progenetrix is still enduring:
The proffered palls, but half-concealed,
The tree, the serpent ever wield
Their immemorial mystic luring.
Forbidden fruit we still implore,
Or Eden Eden is no more.

VIII. 28

Tanya was changed—past recognition!
How she had grown into her role,
The weary pomp of her position
Fused in the substance of her soul!
Who dared to seek the lovelorn maiden
In this assured, decorum-laden
High Priestess of the polished floor?
Yet he had stirred her heart before!
Of him, ere Morpheus' pinions wafted
Down veils of night and slumber brought,
She had with girlish grieving thought,
And, moonbeams in her eyes, had drafted
Some longed-for future, dreamy-dim,
Of walking down life's path with him.

VIII. 29

All ages bow to Love's initial;
But to girls' hearts, the gusts he wields
Are bountiful and beneficial
As rains in springtime to the fields.
The thunderstorms of passion nourish
And freshen growth, they help them flourish,
And life from its eternal root
Adds luscious blossom and sweet fruit.
But when we tread, worn out and fruitless,
The downslope of declining years,
The ghost of passion scarcely cheers:
Thus storms of autumn, bleak and bootless,
But turn green meadows into bog
And shroud the naked woods in fog.

VIII. 30

No doubt—alas! Eugene is vanquished,
In love like any moonstruck lad,
All day with fretful musings anguished,
All night with restless longing sad;
All reason's strictures notwithstanding,
Tatyana's porch, her glass-bound landing
From his attempts are never safe.
He dogs her footsteps like a waif,
Counts it fulfillment worth achieving
To help adjust her stole of furs,
With fevered hand brush over hers,
Platoons of footmen to be cleaving
To make a pathway where she crossed,
Or snatch a handkerchief she lost.

VIII. 31

But she, for all he's taut and harassed,
Ignores him—labor as he may:
At home receives him unembarrassed,
In public has few words to say,
At times inclines her head in greeting,
At others overlooks their meeting.
No vestige of flirtation here—
It does not flourish in her sphere.
Onegin's color starts to fail him:
She fails to notice or—to care;
Onegin shrivels, and for fair,
Ere long consumption must assail him.
All name him doctors near and far—
Who one and all prescribe a spa.

VIII. 32

He stays, though—just to warn his sires
That he'll be joining them eftsoons;
While she, for whose sake he expires,
True to her sex, ignores his swoons.
He perseveres, won't cease from trying,
Is ever hoping, ever vying;
With feeble hand, but greater pluck
Than he had shown in health and luck,
He writes her an impassioned message;
Though by and large he had small use
For letters (not without excuse),
He could not face the next sharp passage
In the progression of his woes;
He wrote; and thus his letter goes:

Onegin's Letter to Tatyana

I doubt not: I shall give offense
By baring secrets dark and painful;
What glances bitterly disdainful
Your haughty eye will now dispense!
What do I seek? For what employment
Do I expose my soul to you?
And how much mischievous enjoyment,
It may be, give occasion to?

When chance that summer willed our meeting—
Though conscious in you of a fleeting
Fondness for me, I would decline
To yield, to let dear habit sway me:
Afraid of love lest it betray me
Of that chill freedom that was mine.
Then a dark shadow fell to blight us:
When Lensky, luckless fate! succumbed,
All tender urges that delight us
I stifled in my breast and numbed.
All ties cast off, as in repentance,
I thought detachment, calm, would pass
In place of happiness. Alas!
How wrong I was; how harsh my sentence!

I know now: always to behold you,
Devoutly follow all your steps,
With loving scrutiny enfold you
When you look up or move your lips;
Be drinking in your voice, be bathing
My soul in all your loveliness,
Writhe in your sight with torment scathing,
Wane, be extinguished—there is bliss!

And I am cheated of such bliss,
My random quest of you pursuing;
Each day I grudge, each hour I miss,
In fruitless pining wasted; ruing
The precious time allowed me yet,
Mortgaged before this by regret.
My span grows short, I need no warning,
But lest it be cut off outright,
I must be certain in the morning
That day will cheer me with your sight . . .

Your bitter virtue may be deeming
My meek entreaty false, I fear,
The subterfuge of wicked scheming;
Your stern rebuke rings in my ear.
But if you knew my mortal anguish—
To be with love's wild fever cursed,
Grope for detachment while I languish,
Sense, while my flesh is parched with thirst;
To long to clutch your knees and, sobbing,
In supplication bent, confess
With pleas, avowals, prayers throbbing,
All, everything I might express;
Instead, with lying self-possession
To armor daily speech and gaze,
Hold converse in well-tempered phrase,
And meet you with a gay expression! . . .

No—come what may, I am unfit
To spite my whole self any longer;
My lot is cast—you are the stronger,
And to your sentence I submit.

VIII. 33

There was no answer. He indited
A second message, then a third.
Still no reply. He is invited
To some assembly, has bestirred
Himself to go, and as he enters . . .
Comes full upon her. How portentous
Her mien! No look or greeting crossed
That zone of January frost!
What worlds of pent-up indignation
These tight lips labor to contain!
Onegin's watchful glances strain:
Where mercy, where commiseration,
What sign of tears? . . . No sign, no trace!
Cold wrath alone shows on this face.

VIII. 34

At most a hint of apprehension
Lest world or husband find a clue
To that misstep too slight to mention
Of which alone Onegin knew . . .
No faintest hope left to be nursing,
Eugene departs, his madness cursing,
And in his gloom all wrapped and furled
Once more retires from the world;
And in his study's lonely stillness
Has leisure to remember well
How in a former worldly spell
Hyp[10] chased him, that malignant illness,
Impaled him on her cruel hook
And hung him in a murky nook.

VIII. 35

Once more he fell to aimless cribbing:
He read Chamfort, he read Rousseau,
He read Manzoni, Herder, Gibbon,
Madame de Staël, Bichat, Tissot;
Of homegrown produce he might bother
To try a sample or another
Between the works of skeptic Bayle
And those of learned Fontenelle.
Fat almanacs we find him scanning,
And journals anxious to instruct,
Where I at one time laurels plucked
And now receive a monthly panning;
To which I answer, now as then,
È sempre bene, gentlemen!

VIII. 36

To what end? While the letters tumbled
Across his sight beyond control,
Desires, dreams, regrets were jumbled
In dense profusion in his soul.
Between the lines of printing hidden,
To his mind's eye there rise unbidden
Quite other lines, and it is these
That in his trance alone he sees.
They were dear tales and droll convictions
Alive among us as of old,
Weird, disconnected dreams untold,
And threats and axioms and predictions,
A spun-out fable's whimsy purl,
Or letters from a fresh young girl.

VIII. 37

And while a drowsy stupor muffles
All thought and feeling unawares,
Imagination deals and shuffles
Its rapid motley solitaires:
He sees on melting snow-sheet dozing
A lad, quite still, as if reposing
Asleep upon a hostel bed,
And someone says: "That's that—he's dead . . ."
He sees old enemies forgotten,
Detractors two-faced and afraid,
A swarm of beauties who betrayed,
A circle of companions rotten,
A rustic house—and who would be
Framed in the window? . . . Who but She!

VIII. 38

Absorbed and wrapped in this employment,
He was about to lose his mind,
Or else turn poet—what enjoyment
That would have yielded all mankind!
I vow: magnetically fired,
My pupil was well-nigh inspired—
Though hitherto distinctly weak—
To cope with Russian verse technique.
What figure, come to think, could better
Suggest a poet, or what scene,
Than in his chimney-nook Eugene,
Forlornly crooning *Benedetta*
Or *Idol Mio*,[11] while the News
Slipped in the fire, or his shoes?

VIII. 39

The days flew; winter had retreated
Before the springtime's melting breath,
And here he was—still undefeated
By verse, or lunacy, or death.
And spring restored some animation:
He breaks his hearthside hibernation
Where, doors and windows tightly closed,
Like a numb marmot he had dozed,
Goes driving through the morning brightness
Down the Embankment in a sleigh:
All gold and blue, the sunbeams play
On brittle floes; the fareway's whiteness
Is thawing into muddy slush,
And through it, whither does he rush,

VIII. 40

Where is it that Onegin hastened?
To his Tatyana—you have guessed!
My wayward hero, still unchastened,
Returned to his quixotic quest.
More like a specter than a mortal,
He seeks her out; finds at the portal
No one to meet him; entrance hall,
Reception room, deserted all.
He tries another door, and winces,
Awe-struck. He sees before him, clad
In simple robe, alone and sad,
Pale cheek cupped in her hand, the princess,
As at a letter-page she peers
And moistens it with silent tears.

VIII. 41

Who at this sight could help surmising
The toll that mute endurance drew,
Princess or no, help recognizing
Poor Tanya—her that once he knew?
Eugene fell at her feet, by boundless
Contrition all undone, while—soundless
But for a shivering start he felt—
She gazed upon him as he knelt
With neither shock nor anger surging . . .
His aspect stricken and distraught,
His eye that pleaded and besought,
She marked them well, and re-emerging,
The heart of old, the dreams that were,
Rose up to live again in her.

VIII. 42

Eyes fixed on him in sightless staring,
She does not beckon him to stand,
Leaves to his greedy lips uncaring
Her limply unresponsive hand.
Who knows what turn her thoughts are taking?
At length, the timeless silence breaking,
Her words come flowing soft and low:
"Onegin, rise. Your state, I know,
Deserves a candid explanation;
Do you remember, far away,
The park, the lane down which that day
Fate led us? How to your oration
I then submitted, meek and dumb?
Today, I think, your turn has come.

VIII. 43

"Why, I was younger then, Onegin,
And prettier, too, for all I know.
I loved you—tell me, to my begging
What answer did your heart bestow,
What comfort, tell me? Cold dissection.
Confess: a little girl's affection,
Shy worship, was no novel thrill!
God! Even now my blood runs chill
When I recall those frigid glances,
That dreadful sermon . . . But no blame
Should touch you: in that hour of shame
You justly dealt with my advances,
You chose a fair, a noble part:
For which I thank you from my heart. . . .

VIII. 44

"Once, in the far-off province yonder,
Remote from busy tongues, allow:
You did not fancy me . . . I wonder
What makes you persecute me now?
What prompts these strange designs upon me?
That now it is incumbent on me
To move in an exalted sphere,
That I have wealth and standing here,
My husband has been maimed in battle,
And we are pets for it at Court?
That now my infamy, you thought,
Would be the universal tattle,
And drawing rooms would pay rich due
Of flattering obloquy to you?

VIII. 45

"I weep . . . If Tanya's erstwhile picture
Still lives in you and pleads for her,
Then know: the wormwood of your stricture,
That wintry speech, I would prefer
(If I could change things in my fashion)
To this dishonorable passion,
And to these letters, and these tears.
For then at least you spared my years,
The adolescence of emotion,
Pitied the callow dreams of youth . . .
But now! What hope led you, in truth,
Here to my feet, what squalid notion?
How could you, with your mind and heart,
Play such a petty, abject part?

VIII. 46

"To me, Onegin, this vain clamor,
This tinsel realm appears inane,
My triumphs here, the modish glamour
In which I dwell and entertain,
All void . . . I would be happy trading
All this pretentious masquerading,
All sound and fume and glossy looks,
For my wild garden, my few books,
For just our humble country dwelling,
For those dear places that I knew
When first, Onegin, I met you,
And for that gentle grassy swelling
Where cross and swaying branches grace
Poor Nanny's final resting place.

VIII. 47

"So close, so begging to embrace it
Was happiness! . . . But now my lot
Is cast for good. If—let me face it—
I acted rashly, blame me not:
My mother, bathed in tears, entreated—
Poor Tanya shrugged, already cheated
Of all she cared about, and so
Was duly married. You must go,
I beg of you as now I leave you.
I know that in your heart abide
A forthright honor, manly pride.
I love you still (yes—why deceive you?),
But I was pledged another's wife,
And will be faithful all my life."

VIII. 48

She left. Eugene stood robbed of motion,
Struck dumb as by a thunderbolt.
Yet in his heart, what stormy ocean
Of feelings seething in revolt!
But presently his ear detected
The ring of spurs, and unexpected,
Tatyana's husband entered. Here,
At a sore pass in his career,
We leave our hero, reader, brother,
For long . . . forever. Far enough
We trailed his wake through smooth and rough.
Let us congratulate each other
Upon the landfall now. Hurray!
And none too soon, you doubtless say.

VIII. 49

My reader—friend or not, whichever
You were—now that the story's end
Is here our mingled paths to sever,
I want to leave you as a friend.
Farewell. Whate'er you sought to capture
In my loose rhymes—be it the rapture
Of reminiscence, pause from toil,
Lively tableaus, the piercing foil
Of wit, or bits of faulty grammar—
Please God you found here but a grain
To conjure dreams, to entertain,
To move the heart, to raise a clamor
Of controversy in the press.
Upon this note we part—God bless!

VIII. 50

You too, strange travel-mate unsteady,
Farewell, and you, my true ideal,
And you, my unremitting, heady,
Though modest toil. You let me feel
All bliss that ever poets covet:
Life in world's storm, yet heedless of it,
And friends' sweet converse by my side.
Ah, many, many days have hied
Since first Tatyana's image hovered,
A cloudy vision, in my mind,
With her Onegin's form outlined,
And when as yet there was discovered
This rambling novel's trend and sense
But darkly in my magic lens.

VIII. 51

But of the trusted band of brothers
To whom the first few quires I read . . .
Some are no more, dispersed the others,[12]
As long before us Saadi[13] said.
Without them was Onegin drafted.
And you, upon whose presence grafted,
Tatyana's form grew animate . . .
Much, oh, so much was snatched by Fate!
Blest he who left in its full glory
The feast of life, who could decline
To drain the brimming cup of wine,
And, loath to finish life's long story,
Abruptly made his parting bow,
As I to my Onegin now.

FINIS

Notes

1. This alludes to Pushkin's adolescent years, spent at Alexander I's exclusive boarding school for young aristocrats, the Lyceum attached to his palace at Tsarskoye Selo near St. Petersburg. There Pushkin wrote his earliest verse and formed lasting friendships with several of the prominent poets and liberals of the late Alexandrine epoch. Stanzas 1–5 are autobiographical reminiscing in the graceful guise of the poet's squiring his Muse from scene to scene of his early amusements, misfortunes, and poetic experiences in the capitals and in exile.

2. This incomplete stanza refers to the famous episode when the grand old man of Russian letters, the poet G. R. Derzhavin, in the last year of his life was a guest at Pushkin's graduation exercises at the Lyceum (1817) and gave praise to the verse recited by the rising young poet who was to outshine him.

3. Lenore—the heroine of Gottfried August Bürger's celebrated ballad by that title, who was claimed by the ghost of her fallen lover and rode to her death in his arms. In his own ballad *The Bridegroom*, Pushkin adopted the breathless meter and evoked the sprightly-macabre atmosphere of Bürger's poem.

4. The evil genius of cold disillusionment who visits the ardent young poet in Pushkin's fragment *The Demon* (1823).

5. The hero of A. Griboyedov's influential play, *Woe from Wit* (1824).

6. Commentators have agreed to insert for the asterisks left here the name of Vice-Admiral A. S. Shishkov, one-time minister of education, an inveterate Slavic purist in the long-drawn controversy over the proper lexical make-up of the emerging literary language.

7. A fictitious name. Guided by Pushkin's album verses and poems of homage, commentators have voiced various conjectures as to the identity of this society beauty.

8. Refers to a decoration in the form of jeweled initials which marked the holder of the court title of *Freylina* (lady-in-waiting, from German *Fräulein*).

9. Saburov, director of the imperial theatres, has been conjectured here as the target intended by Pushkin for the quill of "St.-P.," the caricaturist Count E. C. St. Priest. Prolasov is a cover-name connoting something like "time-server."

10. Hyp or Hip, the Hyps: slangy abbreviations for hypochondria common in English from Swift to about the Regency period, and still listed in Webster. The meaning was close to that of "the blues" or German *Weltschmerz*, the world-weariness or causeless melancholy that was a fashionable predicament of the

gilded youth of the late eighteenth century, a much imitated literary attitude, and especially an element in the curious international syndrome of Byronism. The Russian term was *khandra,* an analogous corruption of the latter portion of the same word, hypochondria.

11. The first words, respectively, of an Italian serenade and a duet refrain popular at the time.

12. This is thought to allude to Pushkin's friends among the executed or exiled Decembrist conspirators of 1825.

13. The great thirteenth-century Persian poet, Muslih-ud-Din Saadi.